DEATH ON LOCATION

DAVID K. WILSON

Cover design by Caroline Johnson

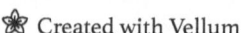 Created with Vellum

1

THE COUPLE RACED through the thick woods, branches slashing against them as they struggled to stay ahead of whatever was behind them.

"Over here!" the man yelled.

He looked back at the woman and could tell she was barely able to stand, much less run.

"You can't give up now," he said.

She shook her head. "I can't."

He reached back and pulled her to him. His white T-shirt was soaked in a mixture of sweat and blood and clung tightly to his muscular body. He held her close and looked into her big blue eyes, pushing her light blonde hair out of her face.

"I'm not losing you," he said. "Not like this."

He put one of her arms over his shoulder to help her walk and they pushed forward as if their lives depended on it. Finally, they burst through the trees into a clearing of tall grass. They stopped and the man looked around in panic.

"Where are they?" he whispered to himself.

Then the trees behind them began to shake. Something was coming. The woman looked back in panic and screamed in sheer terror at what she saw.

"Cut!" a man's voice yelled.

The couple both let out sighs of exhaustion and turned to see what the director wanted this time.

"Love it. It's wild. But still not buying the scream, honey," said Chad McGinnis.

In red cargo shorts and a Hawaiian shirt, Chad looked more like a surfer than a movie director. But, because of the success of his previous film, *Red Moon*, the highest-grossing horror movie of the past decade, he was the hottest director in Hollywood. And he knew it. He ran his hand through his sun-kissed blonde hair, then scratched the matching beard.

"You gotta sell it!" he continued. "It's gotta be big! Operatic!"

"Oh," the woman snarled. "You mean cartoonish."

Chloe Bernard rolled her eyes, making it very clear she was being sarcastic. She had only been in a few movies but had already won a Best Actress Spirit Award and was just as hot a commodity as Chad. From day one of filming *Beneath the Bloody Pines*, she had butted heads with her director's overblown ego and heavy-handed direction.

"I thought that was a great scream," Josh Cole chimed in.

Josh was Chloe's co-star. Tall, lean and ruggedly handsome, he was built to be a movie star. His piercing aqua eyes and rogue Southern drawl only helped seal the deal. He had been a straight-to-cable, romantic comedy staple for years and *Beneath the Bloody Pines* was Josh's first chance to break out of the genre. But if he was feeling the pressure, he sure didn't show it. His big grin and laid-back demeanor were the perfect foil to Chloe's focused drive.

"You think everything's great, Josh," Chad remarked.

Josh replied with a grin and a shrug as the makeup team descended on the actors for touch-ups.

"Don't worry about the sound of the scream," Chad said. "We can fix that in post. But I need to see the scream. When the camera spins around to your face, I need to see full-blown, bug-eyed, shitting-your-pants terror."

He patted her on the shoulder and gave Josh a thumbs up and a wink.

"Oh. I also need your run through the woods to last longer," Chad said. "Go all the way back to the pond and start from there."

The small crew let out a collective groan.

"Come on," Chad said, clapping his hands. "We're gonna lose our light. Let's get to it!"

Josh and Chloe trudged back through the woods. While a movie set with custom-made fake caverns was being used for much of the film shoot, the exterior was being shot at the Cypress River Bottom Wildlife Habitat, several acres of deep pines and swampy ponds nestled in the East Texas woods.

"I don't know if I'm going to make it through this shoot without killing him," Chloe grumbled as she trudged through the woods, swatting a monstrous mosquito away.

"Oh, come on," Josh said. "It ain't that bad."

"I appreciate your optimism," she replied. "But the man's a hack. And these woods are going to eat me alive."

Josh laughed. Having grown up in southeast Texas, the swampy woods made him feel at home. He didn't even mind the intense heat and high humidity.

"Alright. There's the pond," the camera operator said. "Let's just stay out of the mud. Why don't you two start back by that fallen branch?"

The two actors followed the camera operator's direction and walked along the cypress trees that surrounded the swamp. The still water was covered in a slick, green layer of algae and the air was rancid with the smell of mold and earth. But as they got closer to the large fallen branch, they were overtaken by a different foul odor.

"Oh my God," Chloe said. "What the hell is that?"

"Smells like a dead animal," Josh said matter-of-factly. "There's gators in these ponds, you know."

Chloe looked up at Josh to see if he was kidding. She saw the color leave his face.

"Holy shit," he muttered.

She followed his gaze to see what he was looking at. A look of total terror spread across her face as she let out the kind of blood-curdling scream Chad had been asking for earlier.

The camera operator rushed over to see what they were looking at. It was the bloodied stump of a human leg.

2

SAM LAWSON LEANED FORWARD in the chair, staring at the photos, notes, and forensic reports that had taken over an entire wall of his home office. A Texas map hung in the center of the menagerie, littered with red pins that marked the locations of murders. A piece of red string connected each pin to a corresponding victim's photo. A large portion of this evidence was what Ken Mullen had left behind before disappearing.

Ken Mullen was Sam's ex-partner and mentor when Sam had been a detective with the Houston PD. But Sam had transferred to East Texas to lead a quieter life and Mullen eventually retired.

It had been four months since Sam had made the horrifying discovery that Mullen was actually a sadistic serial killer. Dubbed the Replacement Killer because of his penchant for killing a victim only after he had abducted his next victim, Mullen had carried out his murderous spree for years right under Sam's nose. In fact, Mullen had actually asked Sam to help him find the killer and then tried to frame Sam as the serial killer. But Sam was not only able to prove his innocence, he realized the actual murderer was his old friend. But before Sam could arrest his ex-partner, Mullen had slipped away and had not been seen since. In his mad dash to escape, he had left behind a macabre collection of victim photos, mementos, and locations. He had also mailed a note to Sam, both apologizing for his actions and taunting him even further.

I'LL BE SEEING YOU AROUND.

Those were the closing words of the note, and there was no doubt they were meant as a threat. Now, both devastated by his discovery and angered by the betrayal, as well as needing to protect himself and his fiancé, Sam had become obsessed with The Replacement Killer.

Sam's eyes darted back and forth between the different pieces of evidence, looking for something that had yet to jump out at him. As he looked at one evidence photo of a body that had been discovered under a set of wooden stairs, Sam's mind instantly took him back to his first year on the force.

Sam had been a golden child of the Houston Police Department, having risen to the rank of detective by the age of 24. Pumped up with bravado and youthful pride, he would have quickly been eaten alive if he hadn't been fortunate enough to be partnered with seasoned detective Ken Mullen. Mullen saw potential in the young detective and instantly took him under his wing, sharing his experience and knowledge.

Sam remembered the day that he and Mullen had begun the climb of a rear stairwell of a three-floor building in North Houston. As Sam reached out to grab the stair's railing, Mullen playfully slapped it.

"Hands off, Handsy," he said.

"What? I'm not allowed to use the rail?" Sam had asked.

"Fingerprints," Mullen said. "Our perp is probably as much a wuss as you, and there's a good chance he would have grabbed it."

Sam groaned, realizing what Mullen said made half sense.

Mullen looked back at his young partner.

"Get yourself in shape, Pasta Boy," he teased. "In the meantime, use these if you need some help."

He reached down to the horizontal support beams that ran underneath the stair rail.

"Just be sure to grab it so your fingers are on the side facing away from you," he said, demonstrating.

"You look like an idiot," Sam said.

"Well, then start doing some squats, buddy," Mullen said, poking Sam in the stomach.

"Yeah, like you're in better shape than me, old man," Sam said.

"Don't be fooled by this cuddly exterior," Mullen said. "That's for the ladies. But underneath it is a steel fortress. You got a six-pack? I got a keg."

Sam laughed. But he knew Mullen was right. He was a powerhouse that could hold his own against anyone. And, unlike a lot of the older detectives, Mullen wasn't a complete asshole. Sam was lucky to have him as a partner and friend.

"Oh, my God. You could at least crack a window."

Sam jolted back to present day. He had been so lost in his memory he hadn't even noticed Carla had come into the room.

"It's too hot outside," he replied.

Ignoring him, Carla cracked a window anyway.

"You hungry?" she asked. "Want a sandwich or something? Maybe some deodorant?"

Sam smirked. Carla Davenport's dry wit was one of the many things he found irresistible about her. They had recently gotten engaged but hadn't gotten around to setting a date yet. Neither one of them felt a need to rush. They already lived together, so it almost seemed like a formality.

Carla walked over to her fiancé and he slid his arm around her waist. Both of them looked at the horrific wall of death.

"Anything new magically appear?" she asked.

He answered with a sigh.

"Maybe you just need to step away from it for a while," she suggested. "You've been obsessed with nothing but this for three months now."

"Obsessed is a strong word," he half protested.

"The only time you leave this room is to come to bed or to meet with your cop friends and the FBI... to talk about this case."

"He's still out there, Carla," Sam said. "What am I supposed to do?"

Carla climbed into Sam's lap and kissed him gently.

"Let the police do their job," she answered. "That's not you anymore, remember?"

Sam needed the reminder. In an impromptu decision that he refused to regret, Sam had quit the police force and had gotten his private detective license. But Sam had been too busy trying to find Mullen to look for any work. At least when you're a cop, the crime comes to you.

"Did you call that man back?" Carla asked.

"I'm going to," Sam lied.

"You need to," Carla said, standing up. "You need a change

of scenery and we both could use the money. And, come on, it's a movie set. You love movies. Think of how fun that could be."

"I love WATCHING movies. You ever been on a movie set? I used to pull security in Houston for some shoots. Boring as hell."

"True. But this one has a killer and a man-eating alligator in it."

Sam laughed. She had a point.

"I'm calling him for you," Carla said as she stood up. "And don't complain. You're getting a receptionist free of charge."

Sam started to protest, but he knew it wouldn't matter. He also knew Carla was right.

"I'll talk to him," he said. "But no promises about taking the job."

3

SAM WALKED into the large metal warehouse on the outskirts of Quinton. He had driven through a maze of white trailers and trucks stationed in the large parking area in front of the building. Some were large RVs. Some were mobile homes. And others were storage crates connected to big rigs.

The warehouse was where the movie's cavern sets had been built. It also served as ground zero for wardrobe, makeup, and a few production offices. It was buzzing with activity. Crew members pushed lights and other film equipment toward a large room that must have been the set. Wardrobe racks of clothing and bloodied fur costumes lined one wall. People were walking in and out of rooms, shouting instructions at each other. You'd never know that a dead body had just been discovered.

Sam asked someone for directions and was pointed out a side door. There, he found a large luxury mobile home with an open door. And inside was Alan Guzman, the film's producer.

He was immaculately groomed, but very sweaty, and he was yelling into a phone.

"I don't care if it's his daughter's birthday. Get him over here now to fix my air conditioning!"

Guzman looked over his tinted-blue sunglasses and spotted Sam. He waved him inside as he finished the call. He dabbed his forehead with a plush hand towel and stood.

"Sam Lawson, I'm guessing?" he asked. "Alan Guzman. Sorry about the heat. The AC blew. Even it couldn't take the heat."

He spoke fast and flashed a bright, ultra-white smile that reeked of insincerity.

Oh look. A walking douchebag, Sam thought, instantly disliking the man.

"You want some water?" Guzman asked. "Seltzer?"

"Plain water's fine," Sam replied.

"I don't trust plain water."

"Good call. I've been keeping my eye on it for a while," Sam said. "It's definitely up to something."

"Look. They've got me shut out of the woods because of this friggin' investigation," Guzman said, ignoring Sam's joke. "I mean, they got the alligator. Case closed, am I right?"

Even though it had only been a day, Sam was already familiar with the case. It was one of the benefits of Carla being the county coroner.

"From what I understand, the victim is still unidentified. And foul play has not been ruled out," Sam said.

"Look. I get it. There's not a lot going on around here," Guzman said. "You probably don't get a lot of murders. It's exciting. Plus, your medical examiners probably don't have a lot of expertise with these kinds of things."

Sam smirked. "You'd be surprised."

"All I'm saying is, the local cops are making a mountain out of a mole hill. I've shifted the shooting schedule and moving up the interior shots, but I will need to get back out to those woods soon or I'm going to lose a ton of money."

"It's only been a day and a half."

Guzman looked at Sam incredulously.

"And that adds up to a ton of money."

"Look. I came out here as a courtesy," Sam said. "But I honestly don't know what help I can offer. The local PD is on this."

"Can I be frank, Mr. Lawson?" Guzman asked.

"You can be whoever you want," Sam joked. "It's a free country."

"I don't have a lot of faith in your local police force, but you... you've got a pretty impressive reputation."

"To be fair, most of the rumors you probably heard were spread by me," Sam smirked.

"I'd feel much better if you were on the case," Guzman said, still ignoring Sam's attempt to lighten the mood. "And I'm willing to pay you for it."

"The thing is, I'm kind of already involved in a murder investigation," Sam countered.

"I assure you, it will be worth your while," Guzman said. "And if you get this all sewn up in a week, I'll throw in a more-than-generous bonus. You can get back to your other case, AND you'll be a richer man."

Guzman pulled a pen and small notepad from his chest pocket and scribbled down some numbers. He handed the slip of paper to Sam, who had to hide his shock. He had never seen that many zeros in one place.

"I'd also need an advance," Sam said. "To cover expenses."

"Of course," Guzman replied, pulling out a stack of bills. "I'm assuming your type prefers to work in cash. Will $1,000 do?"

Sam nodded, staring at the money. "I can probably work with that."

Both men stood and shook hands.

"You haven't even asked about the movie," Guzman said.

"I've heard it's a Bigfoot movie," Sam said.

"It's MORE than a Bigfoot movie," Guzman corrected. "It's THE Bigfoot movie. You know why no one ever sees Bigfoot? Because he lives underground. A whole race of them. Now, can you imagine getting stuck down there with them? This movie's gonna blow you away. We've got a great cast, a hot director, and it's already getting a lot of buzz. It will make a lot of money for a lot of people IF I can get back in those woods to finish it."

"Well, luckily I'd do just about anything for Bigfoot," Sam said.

"Can I be frank?" Guzman asked again.

"You seem to really want to be Frank," Sam said. "I say go for it."

Guzman ignored him again. Sam couldn't tell if the producer wasn't getting his attempt at humor or if he just didn't care for it.

"I'm going out on a limb hiring local. But my team has advised me that your access to local connections far outweigh your lack of sophisticated investigative tools."

"I completely understand," Sam said. "And my lack of sophistication will not disappoint you."

4

SAM SWUNG OPEN the door to the detective station, his arms spread wide in appreciation of the hero's welcome that would surely be given to him. Instead, he received a few nods and smiles from detectives who were immersed in phone calls, interviewing subjects and commiserating over coffee. Let down by the lack of enthusiasm, Sam turned his attention to the purpose of the visit: Joe Ramirez.

Ramirez was a younger, by-the-book detective who was as close to Sam's opposite as could be imagined. While Sam was on the force, they had their share of run-ins. In fact, Ramirez had even suspected Sam was the Replacement Killer at one point, and even went so far as to have him arrested for the crimes. But as the case progressed, a mutual respect had grown between the two men. In fact, Ramirez had become Sam's main contact as he continued his investigations on Mullen. As luck would have it, he was also the lead detective on the movie set murder.

He spotted the crisply dressed detective talking to a uniformed officer on the other side of the room.

"Yo! Ramirez!" he yelled out.

Ramirez looked up in panic and immediately rushed over.

"Are you crazy?" he said. "What are you doing here?"

"I wanted to talk. This seemed like a good place to find you."

Ramirez hustled Sam back out the door into the stairwell.

"If Bannon sees you here, he'll kill you," he said.

Bannon was the Chief Detective and Sam's former boss. His disdain for Sam was well known and was the main reason Sam had quit the force. It had made Bannon look bad in front of the other detectives and deepened the chief's hatred.

"Bannon's a teddy bear," Sam said. "One look into my sexy eyes and I'll have him eating out of my hand."

"He'll be eating your heart out of your chest. While you watch," Ramirez said. "What do you want?"

"Guess who got hired to investigate a murder?" Sam teased.

Ramirez's shoulders slumped.

"Please, no."

"I'll give you a hint," Sam continued. "It's the only murder case you've got right now."

"You've got to be shitting me."

Sam beamed. "Joe! I thought you'd be more excited. We're gonna be working together again."

"What did I do to deserve this?"

"Oh, stop your moaning," Sam said. "Admit it. You could use the help."

"I'm doing fine, thank you."

"You have any suspects yet?"

Ramirez smirked. "I don't even know who the victim is."

"Yeah. Sounds like you've got this well under control," Sam teased.

Ramirez sighed. "Alright. I could use another set of eyes on this."

"Also, I don't have to tell you that I'm not beholden to the same restrictions you are," Sam said. "That could come in handy."

"No," Ramirez said. "You play by the book. And you feed me any information you find as soon as you find it. Got it?"

"I am your humble servant," Sam said.

"You've never been humble a day of your life," Ramirez chuckled.

"Enough flattery. Catch me up to speed."

"Unfortunately, you probably already know everything I do," Ramirez said. "A leg was found near the Mason Pond at Cypress River Bottom, where they're filming that movie. We caught the alligator and found more body parts inside. But no head. And no hands. So, he's been hard to identify."

"He. So, you know it's a man?"

Ramirez nodded. "Some of the body parts made that very clear, if you know what I mean. But without the head and hands, there's nothing to identify him. And no ID. No missing persons report to check against. Nothing. And this movie has people coming and going every day."

"Time of death?" Sam asked.

"Looks to be between 1 and 2 a.m., Sunday morning."

The stairwell door swung open, and the uniformed officer stuck his head in.

"Ramirez. We just found an unidentified car."

5

THE SILVER JAGUAR COUPE was being pulled out of the stock pond just as Lawson and Ramirez pulled up. Ramirez had been reluctant to have Sam tag along, but then realized he'd show up anyway and, if they were together, Ramirez could keep him on a shorter leash.

Sam whistled in admiration as they approached the car.

"You don't see a lot of those around here," he said.

A uniformed officer approached Ramirez. He was all business until he saw Sam.

"Hey, Sammy," he exclaimed. "I knew you couldn't stay away."

Sam shook the officer's hand.

"You know me, Bobby. How ya doing?"

"Things are great. Haven't seen you at poker in a while. Your old lady doesn't have you all chained down yet, does she?"

The two laughed.

"I hate to break up this reunion, but can we do our jobs for a minute?" Ramirez interjected. "What's the story here?"

Officer Daniels held back a smile, like a kid being caught by a teacher.

"Uh, right," Daniels stammered. "Well, the car was empty. Doesn't look like it was here too long. We'll get it checked for prints and any other evidence."

"A car like that had to belong to one of those movie people," Sam interjected.

"That would be correct. It's a rental and you're not gonna believe who rented it," Daniels said. "Vince Decker."

He looked at Sam and Ramirez for a reaction but got nothing.

"Come on, you gotta know who Vince Decker is," he prodded.

He started humming a TV theme song as a clue.

"Fox Hunt 2000!" Sam exclaimed.

Daniels smiled and nodded.

"That cheesy show from the 90s?" Ramirez asked.

"By cheesy, do you mean classic?" Sam said in fake shock. "Fox Hunt 2000 was the coolest show on TV."

"And Vince Decker was the coolest badass ever," Daniels said.

"He must be in the movie," Sam added.

"Was in the movie," Ramirez said. "It's a pretty safe bet that Mr. Decker is our unidentified gator lunch."

"Why would someone kill an actor?" Daniels asked. "Especially Vince Decker."

"Maybe he did more than just act," Ramirez said. "We'll need to look into his background. See if he was involved with anything else."

"Wait a minute. I worked a case in Houston once. Probably

ten years ago," Sam said. "It was a string of robberies at high-end strip clubs. Guess who owned a couple of them?"

"Get outta here," Daniels said. "Decker ran strip clubs?"

"Very pricy ones," Sam corrected. "He had a couple in Houston, but his home base was Dallas."

"Running that kind of business is sure to get you involved with all types of less than savory people," Ramirez said.

"Where did you say the car was rented from?" Sam asked.

"Emerald Luxury Rentals," Daniels replied. "By the airport."

Sam turned to Ramirez. "So, Decker rented the car at the airport. Which means he flew into town. But Dallas is less than two hours away. Why would someone fly here from Dallas and then rent a car when they could just drive the whole way?"

"By the time you factor in boarding and getting a car, it certainly wouldn't save you any time," Ramirez said.

"Maybe he didn't come from Dallas," Sam said.

He turned to Daniels.

"You need to check all flights that came into Quinton on the day that car was rented. Find out where they came from and who was on them."

"Hey!" Ramirez interjected. "May I remind you that you're not a cop anymore? You don't get to order people around."

Ramirez turned to a confused Officer Daniels, then realized he would say the same thing. He let out a sigh and rolled his eyes.

"Do what he said."

Daniels held back a laugh and nodded.

"Good seeing you, Bobby," Sam yelled out.

"Get your butt back to the poker game," Daniels yelled back. "I need to take your money."

Sam laughed, turning to leave with Ramirez.

"Poker game?" Ramirez asked. "There's a poker game?"

"Yeah, just some of the cops…"

His voice trailed off as he realized the awkwardness of the situation.

"No one's ever told me about a poker game," Ramirez muttered.

"Oh, come on," Sam said. "I bet they have, and you just forgot."

Ramirez shook his head. "No. I'm pretty sure they haven't."

Sam looked at him, unsure of what to do. In a moment of panic, he pulled his phone out of his pocket and put it to his ear.

"Hello? Hey!" he said. "What's up?… Oh, really?"

He motioned to Ramirez that he needed to take the call and walked away for privacy.

"Your phone didn't ring, Lawson," Ramirez said. "I know you're faking it."

Sam looked back at Ramirez, but just pretended harder.

"Seriously? Those bastards," he said as he walked away even faster.

6

RAMIREZ SLID into the red booth across from Sam. In lieu of risking Sam being seen at the police station, Ramirez had arranged to meet him at what he knew was Sam's go-to dining establishment, Jay's Fried Catfish. As expected, Sam jumped at the opportunity and had arrived early enough to finish half his meal already.

"So, are we considering this a date?" Sam asked, slurping his Dr. Pepper through a straw. "I just need to know if you're going to try and kiss me later."

"Did a little digging, and there's no record of Decker on any commercial flights on the day in question," Ramirez said, ignoring Sam's bad joke. "Of course, that doesn't take into account any charter jets."

Sam nodded.

"Well, I did a little digging myself," he said. "And I did account for charter jets. In fact, that's what I focused on."

He grinned at Ramirez.

"Come on. A guy like Decker's not flying commercial."

Sam popped a piece of catfish in his mouth. He chewed slowly, making Ramirez wait.

"So?" Ramirez finally asked. "What did you find?"

Sam nodded, holding up a finger to tell Ramirez to wait a little longer. Ramirez groaned in frustration and Sam, enjoying the suspense he was creating, took a little extra time to chew. Finally, he spoke.

"There were three charter jets that came in on Tuesday," he said. "One belonged to a local optometrist. Another to a Dallas businessman. And the third was leased by the studio that's making the movie.

"Our movie?" Ramirez asked.

"You know of any other movie filming in town?" Sam asked. "But wait. There's more."

He pulled out his phone and gave it to Ramirez.

"Airport security footage shows someone that looked a lot like Decker walking off of that plane. And he wasn't flying alone."

Sam reached over and scrolled through several pictures, stopping at one in particular.

"Is that the producer?" Ramirez asked.

"Alan Guzman. In the slimy flesh," Sam said. "And it gets better."

He scrolled to another photo. In it, Guzman and Decker appeared to be arguing.

"Decker and Guzman may have traveled together, but it certainly wasn't the friendly skies. They were having a serious disagreement."

"We need to get a copy of that flight's manifest," Ramirez said.

"Or we can just go talk to Guzman," Sam said. "Why wait in line at the fountain when you can go straight to the well?"

Ramirez shook his head.

"Some of us still need to play by the rules, Lawson."

"Talking to Guzman isn't breaking any rules," Sam countered.

"You've got to love this P.I. stuff. Now you can take all the shortcuts you want and no one can call you out on it," Ramirez said.

"You sure do seem to be trying," Sam grinned back.

Ramirez shrugged.

"Honestly? I'm probably just jealous," he said.

Then he leaned forward.

"Something I've been dying to ask you. This whole thing with Mullen and how it went down and then you quitting. I didn't contribute to that, did I?"

"What?" Sam asked. "No. It wasn't you. It was Chief Bannon riding my ass. And all the crap that was getting in the way of me doing my job."

"There's a reason for the rules," Ramirez said. "You know that, right?"

"I've got no problem with rules that protect the innocent," Sam said. "I have an issue with the rules that do nothing but protect the police brass. Lots of cover-my-ass regulations that serve no purpose but allow our duly elected officials stay elected."

Ramirez nodded.

"Yeah. I hear ya."

"We need both of us," Sam said. "I've got to push the system and you've got to pull me back in."

"Kind of hard to do when you quit the force on us," Ramirez said.

Sam shrugged and winked.

"Nah. I just made it easier for you to arrest me when I screw up."

7

RAMIREZ AND SAM walked through the movie production warehouse toward Guzman's office trailer.

"You know, we're not partners," Ramirez said. "You shouldn't even be here."

"I'm here to help," Sam said. "An extra set of eyes."

They walked past a garment rack holding several furry Bigfoot costumes.

"I could put one of these on and go undercover," Sam said. "I'll just blend into the background, and you won't even know I'm here."

"Why do I find that impossible to believe?" Ramirez grumbled.

As they neared the trailer, they could hear two men yelling inside. It stopped immediately when Ramirez knocked on the door. After a few muffled grumblings, the door flung open and a man in his mid-twenties stormed out. His face was red from anger, and he was clearly still fuming.

"Pardon Mr. Fowler," Guzman said from within the trailer. "Temperamental writer. I swear, I spend more time babysitting the egos of these people than anything else."

Sam looked back to watch Fowler storm through the studio. The writer punched the rack of Bigfoot costumes in frustration. But he missed the wooly fabric and hit the metal pole of the rack instead. The writer grabbed his hand in pain and Sam watched as his moment of rage dissolved into embarrassing humility. Regaining his footing, Fowler stomped out of the warehouse, angry and embarrassed.

"What'd you do to piss him off?" Sam asked.

"He'll be fine. This shutdown is costing us plenty, so I've had to make some budget cuts," Guzman explained, seeming nonplussed by the altercation. "I asked him to rewrite some scenes to something we can afford. He starts screaming about 'the art.'"

Guzman laughed as he directed the men to a couple of chairs opposite a makeshift desk.

"I see you got your AC working," Sam said.

"Yes, and please shut the door behind you to keep out that god-awful heat. I don't know how you people live with it."

"Can I get his name again?" Ramirez asked, pulling out a notepad.

"The writer? His name is Richard Fowler," Guzman said. "Great writer but a pain in the ass. So, are you here to tell me you've solved the case and I can get back to work?"

"Not entirely. Although we have made progress," Ramirez said. "But I could use your help in clearing up a bit of confusion. Did you fly in on a charter jet this past Tuesday?"

"Yes. I had gone back to L.A. for a meeting on Friday and came back Saturday morning."

"Can you tell me who else was on that flight?" Ramirez asked.

Guzman studied the two men, trying to figure out what they were getting at.

"Vince Decker was with me."

"Anyone else?" Ramirez asked.

"The crew. One lovely flight attendant with legs to die for. Pilot and co-pilot," Guzman said. "Why do you ask?"

"You and Decker got into a bit of an argument," Sam interjected. "Was it about the rewrites, too?"

Ramirez glared at Sam, silently chastising him for interjecting.

"We had a disagreement," Guzman said. "Vince is a bit of a hothead, but he gets over it quick."

"When was the last time you saw Mr. Decker?" Ramirez asked.

"That morning. At the airport. He's not expected on set until the end of the week. Can you tell me what you're getting at here?"

"What were you two arguing about, Mr. Guzman?" Ramirez asked. "You seemed as upset as he did."

On cue, Sam pulled out the airport security photos showing the two men arguing. Guzman studied the pictures. Sam could almost hear the producer's brain whirring to come up with an explanation.

"That looks like more than an actor upset about his lines," Sam remarked.

Guzman looked up at Sam.

"I hired you," he said. "You work for me. What the hell are you doing?"

"You hired me to find the truth and that's all I'm trying to do," Sam said. "No one is accusing anyone of anything."

"Answer my question, Mr. Guzman," Ramirez said. "What were you two arguing about?"

Guzman let out a sigh. "Money. What else?"

"He wanted more money?" Sam asked.

"He wanted his money back," Guzman said. "Decker isn't just an actor in the film, he's a producer and investor. He's put up a lot of money to help get this film made."

"And he wanted it back?" Ramirez asked.

Guzman laughed.

"Yeah. Can you believe it? I mean, the asshole is in the business. He knows how it works. But he caught a ride with me back from L.A. and told me something had come up and he needed his money back. I reminded him his money had already been spent. Equipment. Salaries. Location fees."

"How much are we talking about?" Sam asked.

"He put in a hundred Gs," Guzman said. "Wanted it all back. Every penny."

"I bet it pissed him off when you said no," Sam said.

"He panicked," Guzman said. "Totally flipped out. Demanded I give him his money back immediately. I told him I'd be happy to, but I just didn't have it. I offered him a ride to the hotel, but he said he was going to get his own car. He had some things he needed to do. And that's how I left him."

Guzman leaned forward.

"Why are you so interested in me and Decker?" he asked.

"Because we believe Decker is the one who was murdered," Ramirez said.

"Holy shit," Guzman said, leaning back in shock. "Are you sure?"

"We can't say definitively, but it's a pretty safe bet," Ramirez said. "Do you know anyone who would want him dead? Anyone that was angry at him? Maybe over money?"

Guzman looked at the two men.

"You think I did it?" he asked. "You seriously think I killed him?"

"We're just trying to get information," Ramirez said.

"If I did it, why would I hire you?" Guzman asked Sam. "And by the way, I needed him in this movie. I needed his retro star power. That's very marketable these days. And I needed his money."

"But he was threatening to take it back," Sam said.

"He was asking me to give it back," Guzman corrected. "And I said no. He couldn't take it back if he wanted to. We had contracts."

Guzman's mind was spinning. He grabbed a walkie-talkie on his desk.

"Erin, get in here. And call my lawyer," He looked at Sam and Ramirez. "I've got to contain this. Get the entire crew to sign NDAs so we can keep this under wraps."

"NDAs?" Sam asked.

"Yeah. Non-Disclosure Agreements. So they can't talk to the press."

"I know what they are. But can you do that?" Sam asked.

"If they want their paycheck, they'll sign. We'll stipulate that it's until an arrest is made. Then they can run to TMZ as fast as they want."

"Why do you want to keep them quiet?" Sam asked.

"To keep the press out of it," Guzman answered. "If they start showing up, we'll have to completely shut down. If this gets out now, it could tank the movie."

Ramirez wasn't interested in Guzman's damage control.

"Mr. Guzman, you said he panicked when you told him no," Sam said.

"Huh? Yeah. Major flip out," Guzman said.

"Like he owed someone money," Sam said to Ramirez.

"Someone he was afraid of," Ramirez replied. "Mr. Guzman, do you know if Decker was in debt to anyone? Have any associations with someone who would be threatening to him?"

"I'm assuming you know about his business, right?" Guzman asked. "Look. Money is money to me. I don't discriminate. So, when Decker wanted to invest in this movie - with the price of also being cast in it - I didn't balk and I didn't ask questions. I don't know anything about his financial picture, but I can tell you that when you get involved in adult entertainment, you're gonna rub shoulders with some people you don't want to piss off."

A young woman knocked on the trailer door.

"Erin, come in. Gentlemen, I've got a big fire to put out. And can I please beg you to keep Decker's name out of the press?"

"We can't do that, Mr. Guzman," Ramirez said.

"Please. I'll tell the crew to cooperate fully with you, but just no press. Not yet."

Ramirez looked at Sam then back to Guzman.

"I'll try. But no promises."

Guzman started speaking to Erin in hushed tones before Sam and Ramirez even stepped out of the trailer. They were met immediately by Chad, the director.

"Mr. Lawson. Just the man I was looking for."

Sam looked at Ramirez then back to the director.

"Oh. I already met the detective. So... process of elimination. I'm Chad McGinnis. The director. Can I borrow you for a minute?"

Ramirez eyed him suspiciously.

"Don't worry. It's not related to the case," Chad said.

8

RAMIREZ HAD OFFERED to wait in the car, but Chad told him that he'd have a car take Sam back to the station when they were done. Ramirez reluctantly left Sam with the director, but not before telling him to keep him in the loop if he received any pertinent information.

"Is this the part where you offer me the lead in your movie?" Sam asked.

Chad laughed.

"Yeah, right," Chad said. "Can you imagine? Just for curiosity's sake, though... You ever act before?"

Sam laughed as Chad led him through the warehouse. As they walked, Sam craned his neck to see if anything was being filmed. Chad noticed.

"No shooting today," he said. "We're still putting the finishing touches on some of the sets to start tomorrow. That dead body threw everything off."

They walked out of the warehouse where a black town car was waiting. Chad opened the rear door for Sam then walked around to the other side. Sam slid into the back seat and looked at the driver. He was a small man, barely tall enough to see over the steering wheel. He looked back at Sam through the rear-view mirror.

"Take us to the hotel, would you, Marty?" Chad asked as he shut his car door. "This is Guzman's car, but he won't mind. Right, Marty?"

Chad laughed. Marty didn't even crack a smile.

The office trailer was in a section of the Quinton Forest Preserve that had been approved for the film production, which meant Sam had a fifteen-minute drive to get some information from Chad. He just had to be careful to not let him know Decker was the suspected victim.

"It's Decker isn't it?" Chad said.

"Decker? Who's Decker?" Sam bluffed.

"I can't get hold of him and you guys are sniffing around, talking to Guzman," Chad said. "It's ain't rocket science."

He slumped in his seat.

"Jesus, this could kill the movie."

He looked at Sam and realized how selfish that sounded.

"And, of course, my heart goes out to Decker's family. Does he have a family?"

Sam told Chad the body hadn't been officially identified, but Decker seemed to have disappeared. He decided not to tell him about Decker's rental car. No sense fanning the flames. Chad didn't offer anything else that was very helpful. He hadn't seen Decker since a scene conference Friday afternoon. He said Decker seemed jittery, but he just figured he was coked up.

"So, Decker was involved in drugs?" Sam asked.

Chad shrugged and laughed.

"Dude, calm down. I just figured that. Nothing else."

The car finally pulled into the parking lot of the Chateau of the Pines hotel.

"We wanted to stay at the Marriott, but it's on the far side of town," Chad explained as they got out of the car. "This is the closest thing Guzman could find that would keep our actors happy. Personally, I could've slept in my trailer."

Chad led Sam through the lobby and out to the swimming pool.

"We rented out the entire hotel, thinking it would be an in-and-out shoot," Chad explained. "This has got to be costing a small fortune."

With the movie on hold while they shifted locations, much of the cast and crew dealt with the East Texas heat by sitting around the pool. Sam scanned the crowd for any celebrities and immediately recognized Chloe Bernard. He gulped. Even though he had seen her in movies and on talk shows, he was still startled at how beautiful she was. He was also slightly stunned at the barely-there bikini she was wearing. It was going to take all of his will power not to stare. Or drool. Or even speak.

Relaxing in the lounge chair next to her was Josh Cole. Sam didn't recognize him but could tell he was a movie star. He instinctively sucked in his stomach at the sight of Josh's washboard abs. On the other side of Josh, sheltered under an umbrella, was another woman with dark hair and large red sunglasses that hid her face. Still, Sam could tell she was beautiful and most likely another actress. They looked like Greek gods taking a break from Mount Olympus to spend the day slumming with mortals.

Aren't they supposed to look normal in real life? Sam wondered to himself.

"Sam, I want you to meet Chloe Bernard, Josh Cole and Ana Ford, the three leads in our movie," Chad said. "This is Sam Lawson, the private detective helping to get us back on track."

Chloe smiled warmly and extended her hand.

"Nice to meet you, Mr. Lawson."

"Sam. You can call me Sam," Sam heard himself mutter.

Josh jumped up, surprising Sam with his nervousness.

"So, you're THE Sam Lawson?" Josh asked. "I'm a big fan."

He shook Sam's hand enthusiastically, and realizing Sam's confusion, explained himself.

"I've read up on you. Doing research for the movie. I play a cop and... wait. Did he say you're a private detective?"

Sam explained how he had left the force recently to strike out on his own.

"I have a problem with red tape," he offered. "And authority figures."

"Sounds like someone else I know," Ana teased with a smile, poking at Josh's leg.

Ana lowered her glasses to reveal brilliant green eyes and Sam became immediately lost in them. He was pulled back to reality by Chad's voice. Talk about a buzz kill.

"I need to borrow Josh for a few minutes, ladies," Chad said.

Josh grabbed a polo shirt and followed Chad and Sam into the lobby.

"Sam, meet your new partner," Chad said.

Sam looked at Josh, who was beaming like an excited Golden Retriever.

"I don't understand," Sam said.

"Josh is playing a Texas detective and you happen to be that very same thing," Chad explained. "Josh thought it would be a good idea to shadow you for a while. And I agree."

Sam shook his head.

"No. Sorry," Sam said. "And no offense, Josh. But I don't play well with others. It's bad enough I've got to trail Ramirez around."

"You won't even notice me," Josh said. "I'll be like a pet rock. Just sitting there. Watching. Taking notes."

"Yeah. That's even creepier," Sam said. "I'm gonna have to pass."

"I don't want to pull rank, man. But may I remind you that you work for Guzman, which means you work for the movie," Chad said. "I ran this past him and he's on board. If you don't like it, he'll hire a PI who does. His words, not mine."

"Come on, Sam," Josh said. "It'll be great. You can bounce ideas off of me. I can offer my theories. Give you a fresh perspective. Two brains are better than one, right?"

Sam sighed. What he wanted to do was walk away. But Carla would kill him if he did. And it was a lot of money.

"Alright, but I call the shots, not you," Sam said to Josh, who was bouncing in place like a kid who was just told he was going to Disney World. "You don't get a gun. And you are not allowed to go into any place that I feel is dangerous."

"Insurance wouldn't allow for those things anyway," Chad replied. "Alright then! A partnership is formed."

"It is not a partnership," Sam corrected. "It's a dictatorship. You have to do as I say and that means staying out of the way as much as possible."

"You gotta deal, Dictator Sam," Josh said with a grin. "Just let me go change."

"What? Right now?" Sam asked.

"No time like the present," Josh said, slapping a speechless Sam on the shoulder. "Let's go solve a murder."

9

WITH HIS NEW ACTOR/PARTNER in tow, Sam decided it was time to visit the morgue. He had several reasons. First, he wanted to check with the coroner to see if she had any new information on their victim, now identified as Vince Decker. Secondly, since the coroner was his fiancé, he'd get a chance to say hello. Finally, he was hoping that a visit to a room full of corpses and mutilated body parts would be enough to convince Josh that maybe he wouldn't want to tag along after all.

Sam held his breath as he pushed open the double doors to the morgue — a habit he picked up years ago and had no intention of ever breaking. It wasn't that the morgue stunk. It was just that it had a unique chemical smell that Sam associated with death. He was hoping the odor would catch Josh off guard but was disappointed when the actor appeared completely unfazed.

Carla was doing paperwork at her desk as the pair walked in. When she saw Sam, she let herself smile for just a second. She tried not to smile much at work. Having a stoic, professional demeanor helped get the good ol' boy network to take her a little more seriously.

"Well, they'll let anybody in this building," she teased.

"I told them I knew the Dead Body Lady," Sam teased back.

As Carla stood, she noticed Josh. It was the first time Sam had truly seen her shocked.

"This is..." Sam started.

"Josh Cole," Carla interrupted. "Oh, I know who you are."

She jutted out her hand enthusiastically.

"I am such a fan," she gushed.

Josh flashed his perfect smile.

"Well, that's always good to hear," he said.

"*Love in Louisiana. Second Chances. New England Nights*," Carla said. "I've seen them all."

"There's been a lot," Josh replied.

"You know all those romance movies I watch," Carla explained to Sam. "Mr. Cole is in pretty much every one of them. Or at least my favorites."

"You're the chick flick guy," Sam said to Josh in recognition.

"That's been my bread and butter," Josh said, slightly embarrassed. "But I'm looking to expand my horizons. That's why this role is important to me."

"Josh is in the movie they're filming," Sam said to Carla. "I'm going to let him shadow me for a day or two to get a feel for what a real detective does."

"Whoa, is that a dead body?" Josh asked, walking past the couple to a corpse laid out on an examining table.

"Josh Cole?" Carla mouthed to Sam.

"Cool your jets," Sam mouthed back.

Carla winked and turned to Josh and the corpse.

"That's Lenny Tubble," she said. "Looks like he died of a heart attack. I just need to make it official."

"How can you tell it was a heart attack?" Josh asked.

"Hate to break up Death 101," Sam interrupted. "But we came here for a reason."

"And your timing is perfect," Carla said, rolling Lenny's table back into his chamber of the refrigerated cabinet.

She opened another chamber and pulled out the slab. A white cloth covered the contents and Carla casually whipped it down to reveal several half-eaten body parts. Sam felt a wave of nausea but held it in. He looked at Josh, who leaned forward in fascination.

"This is amazing," he said. "Is this all that's left of him?"

"All that we found in the alligator," Carla said. "They're still dredging the pond for other body parts. Part of the reason your movie is shut down."

"No head, huh?" Josh asked as he studied what looked to be part of a human torso.

"Not yet, but I was able to find enough of a finger to corroborate your suspicions," she said to Sam. "This is definitely Vince Decker."

Sam looked at Josh, who was lost in his fascination.

"Did you know Mr. Decker?" Sam asked.

"Not really," Josh said. "Met him at the table read, but he wasn't on the call sheets for another couple of days. So, an alligator can do all of this?"

"Actually, he got some help," Carla said as she slid on a pair of latex gloves.

She picked up a foot and pointed at the severed end.

"Looks like Mr. Decker's body was sawed up first and then fed to the alligator," she said.

Sam and Josh leaned in at the same time, bumping heads. They both backed away awkwardly.

"How can you tell?" Josh asked.

Carla picked up a couple of body parts and showed the edges to Josh. Sam's instinct was to turn his head and gag, but with his fiancé and her matinee idol watching, he played it tough. Still, he could feel beads of sweat forming on his forehead.

"The muscle tissue was severed, not torn apart. It's the same for each body part," she explained. "And it's amateur work. Nothing surgical about it."

"Any way you slice it, we have a murder on our hands," Josh said with dramatic flair.

"And the killer is a bit of a cut-up," Sam added, just as dramatically.

The two men looked at each other in a moment of mutual admiration.

"Oh, dear God. There are two of you now," Carla muttered. "I also found this in the alligator's stomach."

The two men turned their attention to a plastic bowl of mangled and chewed items. It looked like a watch, a chewed-up condom wrapper, and some change. Sam motioned for Carla to pick up a partial piece of paper. It looked like part of a business card. The only legible portion was the last few letters of a name:

RRETT

Sam pulled out his wallet and fumbled through his business cards until he found what he was looking for. He held it up next to the mangled piece. The paper and type matched. So did the last five letters of the name.

JIMMY GARRETT

"That's the same card," Josh said.

Sam nodded. "Looks like Vince Decker and I know someone in common."

10

CARLA CONTINUED to act casual as Sam and Josh left the morgue. She tried not to check out the way Josh fit in his tight blue jeans by focusing on the pieces of a human body laid out in front of her. Talk about a distraction. But she did steal one final glance as both men walked out the door.

She felt her face grow warm and flush and was immediately embarrassed when John Doyle, the Assistant Examiner, walked into the morgue. She looked down at Vince Decker's remains and pretended too hard to be studying them.

"Who's that guy with Sam?" Doyle asked.

"I don't know. Some actor," Carla bluffed. "He's following Sam around for a few days."

"So, what were they doing here?" Doyle asked. "Is Sam working the Gator case?"

Carla filled Doyle in on Sam's role in the investigation, as well as the discovery of their victim's identity.

"His name is Vince Decker," she said. "He's an actor and businessman."

"No way," Doyle said. "Vince Decker? Fox Run 2000 Vince Decker? Holy shit."

He walked over and looked at the anonymous body parts with newfound interest.

"I heard all those people from the movie are staying at the hotel by the highway," he said. "Did you know Chloe Bernard is in it?"

"Who's Chloe Bernard?" Carla asked with very little real interest.

"Uh, my next wife," Doyle replied. "Seriously. She's gorgeous. And a friend of mine works at the hotel. Says she spends most of her time lying by the pool in a bikini. Always under an umbrella. So she don't get sunburned, I'm guessing."

"Maybe you can get a second job as the pool boy," Carla teased. "Certainly be more useful than you are here."

Doyle smirked and nodded.

"How's Mr. Tubble doing?" he asked as he slipped on a pair of latex gloves.

"Patiently waiting for you," Carla replied. "I need to get some fresh air. You want some coffee? My treat."

SHE COULD HAVE CUT through the police station parking lot but decided to prolong her errand and walk around the building. Even though it was still a typical hot and humid day, she loved the feel of the sun on her skin. As she walked, she thought about which friend she should text first to tell who she had just met. She laughed at herself. Carla was a pragmatist and realist and had met many celebrities over the years. She was not easily star struck. Still, she couldn't deny she felt giddy as a schoolgirl.

I mean, it's Josh Cole!

She decided on a group text and began typing into her phone as she walked.

FROM HIS VANTAGE point behind some bushes on the other side of the street, he watched her every move. The bounce in her step. The smirk as she typed. He could tell she was light and carefree.

Good, he thought. *She's letting her guard down.*

Then his attention was diverted by a young woman stepping out of the front door of the police station. He recognized her immediately. Her name was Jasmine, and she was one of the sex workers that frequented the string of no-tell motels along the north loop.

He felt the excitement pulse through every vein in his body and the familiar cloud of hunger and obsession overtake him.

It's almost time.

11

"Jimmy Garrett is a prominent Quinton businessman," Sam explained to Josh as they drove to pay a visit to the man whose business card was found inside the alligator. "Made his name in the oil business."

"Ahh. And you think Vince Decker was trying to get into the oil business, too," Josh said.

"Not necessarily. Garrett is also what you in the movies would call a drug kingpin," Sam said. "He pretty much runs the drug trade in Northeast Texas, Louisiana and parts of Arkansas."

"If you know that, why don't you just arrest him?" Josh asked.

"Knowing it and proving it are two different things," Sam said. "We've been trying to build a case against him for years, but he's got just about everyone in his back pocket. We were close once, but then we got pressure from the State Attorney's office to back off. They claimed they were deep into a federal sting against Garrett, but it was a lie. Nothing ever happened."

"So, you think Vince was buying drugs from this guy?"

"Possibly, but I don't think that's it. Garrett's also a pretty ruthless loan shark."

"Jesus," Josh said. "Is there anything this guy DOESN'T do?"

Sam laughed.

"He's what we call a 'serial entrepreneur.' A real go-getter."

"So, how do you want to play this?" Josh asked. "You want me to question him while you sneak through his house looking for evidence?"

"This ain't the movies, Josh. And you're questioning no one. You are here to observe and that's it."

Josh started to protest but Sam quickly shifted the subject.

"I have to ask you. Most people have a less than pleasant experience when they go to a morgue and a lot of them get sick when they see a dead body. It was no big deal for you."

Josh grinned.

"I played a medical examiner in *Buried Feelings*. I like to research my characters—like I'm doing now—and I may have visited a few morgues along the way."

"How many of those movies have you made?" Sam asked.

"Medical examiner movies?"

"Romantic comedies."

"I take it you're not a fan?" Josh asked.

"You've seen one, you've seen them all," Sam replied. "No offense."

"Yeah. There's definitely a formula to them. But I try to bring something unique to every performance."

"You ever not get the girl?"

Josh grinned. "Oh, I always get the girl."

Sam chuckled. "I bet you do."

He pulled his truck off the main road and stopped at a tall iron security gate.

"What the hell?" he muttered. "How did he even know?"

The men looked through the iron bars of the gate. Behind it sat a massive, Spanish Colonial mansion, complete with a red tile roof and rustic, stucco walls. A large circular driveway encircled a six-foot-tall mermaid water fountain and was lined with a Jaguar, a large black SUV and Joe Ramirez's red Honda Civic.

12

"CAN I HELP YOU?" a voice asked through the speaker next to the gate.

Sam looked at the security camera pointing at him and instinctively reached for his badge—always a guaranteed entry pass—when he realized he no longer carried one.

"I'm here to see Mr. Garrett," Sam said. "Sam Lawson. I'm with Detective Ramirez. The cop who's already here."

There was a long pause as the person on the other end of the speaker probably checked Sam's story.

"I'm sorry," the voice finally replied. "Who did you say you were again?"

Before he could reply, Josh leaned over so that he was more visible to the security camera.

"Hey there. I'm Josh Cole. The actor? I've been in a lot of movies. You can look me up. I was hoping Mr. Garrett could spare five minutes. I'm preparing for a role, and I'd love his insights."

Another long pause. Finally, the voice spoke again.

"Lean closer so I can get a better look at you."

Josh grinned and winked at a slightly stunned Sam, leaning over him so his face could be more easily seen. Another minute passed and then the iron gate began to open. Sam looked at Josh, who shrugged.

"You'd be surprised who watches my movies," he said.

BEFORE SAM COULD EVEN KNOCK on the massive mahogany door, it swung open, and a giant man stepped out. He was tall and muscular, which was accentuated by his skin-tight black T-shirt. But it was the glare in his eyes and scowl on his face that made him intimidating. Without the slightest hint of emotion, he motioned for Sam and Josh to raise their hands and they both did so without hesitation. Having been here before, Sam had expected the pat down and had left his pistol in his truck. He could have warned Josh but thought it would be more fun if he was caught by surprise. Much to his disappointment, Josh grinned through the whole search.

"Sorry about your welcome committee," a voice came from inside the house.

Jimmy Garrett was walking toward them. He was a tall man, dressed casually in an untucked denim shirt, jeans and brown cowboy boots. Clean cut with casually tousled salt and pepper hair, he looked more like an aging cowboy than a renowned businessman and ruthless drug lord.

"This is Hector. He's my chief of security," Garrett continued. "There are a lot of crazy people out there."

Garrett walked directly to Josh, practically ignoring Sam.

"I can't believe Josh Cole is standing in front of me," he said. "My wife is gonna juice her jeans."

He shook Josh's hand vigorously. "It is a pleasure to meet you, Mr. Cole. Please come in. You want some tea?"

"Tea sounds great," Sam said loudly, trying to insert himself into the conversation.

Garrett put an arm around Josh's shoulder and led him down the hallway, peppering him with questions about specific movies. Sam followed awkwardly, unsure if Garrett even knew he was there. They all walked into a spacious room with beamed, cathedral ceilings. The far wall was floor-to-ceiling glass, offering a panoramic view of the landscaped backyard and swimming pool. In the center of the room, two black leather couches were positioned in an L-shape around a large, square wooden coffee table. It was a home right out of Interior Digest and, even though Sam had seen it before, it still blew him away.

Standing next to one of the couches was a scowling Ramirez. He glared at Sam, letting him know he was unwanted. Sam smiled and waved at the detective.

"Hey, Ramirez," he said. "Sorry we're late. Got hung up in traffic."

"So, you're still working together even though you... retired?" Garrett asked.

"Oh, I'm far from retired," Sam replied. "Me and Ramirez are practically partners. Honestly, Garrett, I'm honored you keep up with my career."

"I'm one of the few people that still reads the paper," Garrett said.

He motioned for the men to sit down. Sam and Ramirez were on one couch. Garrett and Josh on the other. Hector stood menacingly in the foyer between the men and the front door. Garrett turned his attention back to the movie star.

"I'll be honest, my wife is the one that's a big fan of your movies," he said. "But I'll be damned if I don't get sucked in every time. What was that one where you were a park ranger and you got stuck in the woods with that woman?"

"*Love Gone Wild,*" Josh answered.

"How did you do that fight with the bear?" Garrett asked. "I mean, that looked real as shit. Was it CG?"

"No, sir. That was a real bear," Josh said. "But he was trained, and it wasn't me. A stunt double, wearing protective gear did the heavy lifting. I just did the close-ups with a man in a bear suit."

Garrett laughed hard. It was a loud laugh that echoed in the large room.

"No shit?" he asked.

"Movie magic," Josh said.

"Mr. Garrett," Ramirez interrupted. "I know your time is valuable, but I still have a few questions."

"My Lord. What else do you want to know? I told you I never met the fella. If I did, I'd most certainly brag about it. And if he owed me money, why would I have him killed? He can't pay me back that way. That's a fool's move."

He turned back to Josh.

"You had to have been thrilled to get to work with THE Vince Decker," he said.

"Yes, sir. I was," Josh replied. "Unfortunately, I barely even got to meet him before he was killed."

"That's a real shame," Garrett said. "You're too young, but back in our day, Vince Decker was the shit."

"Mr. Garrett, I'm sorry but I have to ask," Ramirez interrupted again. "Can you tell me where you were Tuesday night between midnight and 3 a.m.?"

Garrett sighed. "I don't know. Sleeping? Playing poker with the boys? Having a late-night dinner with the mayor? I've got an airtight alibi. Take your pick."

"Could you be more specific?" Ramirez asked.

"I cannot. But my lawyer can. And any other talking you need to do, you can go through him."

He stood, signaling that the interview was over.

"Mr. Cole, you will have to come for dinner sometime," Garrett said, shaking his hand. "When my wife finds out I met you and she didn't, I may be next in line for gator food.

He laughed loudly again.

"Would you mind if I got a picture?" he asked.

Josh looked at a very annoyed Sam and Ramirez and shrugged as Garrett motioned at Hector to bring him his phone. He held it up and put his arm around Josh, smiling for the selfie.

"You want me to take it for you?" Sam asked.

Caught up in the moment, Garrett happily handed his phone to Sam.

"Move over by this wall, so you don't have the light at your back," Sam instructed.

As Garrett moved Josh to another spot, Sam held the camera up. But instead of framing the picture, he was scrolling through Garrett's photos. As expected, he quickly found a picture of Garrett posing with Vince Decker.

"Say cheese," Sam said as he discreetly switched the phone back to camera mode.

13

SAM'S black Ford F-150 followed Ramirez's Civic around the circular driveway and back out through the gates.

"He seemed like a nice enough guy," Josh said. "Hard to believe he's all those things you said."

"Don't let looks deceive you," Sam said. "Bad guys aren't all black hats and twirly moustaches. Most of 'em blend right in. Normal is their camouflage."

"Ooh. That's good," Josh pulled out a notepad from his back pocket. "Normal is their camouflage. Mind if I use that?"

Sam smiled. "Only if you follow it with, 'As the wise Sam Lawson once said'."

"Yeah. I'll be sure to slip that in."

Sam turned off the busy road, opting for a side road with less traffic. Even if it took him longer, Sam hated standing still in traffic or at red lights. A result of his years spent dealing with Houston's gridlock.

"Tell me what you know about Vince Decker," he said.

Josh shrugged. "I don't know much. Like I said, I only met him those couple of times. He was alright."

"He was alright?" Sam asked. "No. This is not the time to respect the dead. I need it raw."

"Ok. Well. Honestly, he was kind of a jerk to me. Kind of a jerk to everyone."

"What kind of jerk?" Sam asked. "Did he yell at people? Ignore people? Get into arguments? Jerks come in lots of flavors. More and more every day."

"He acted like he was better than everyone and was pissed when no one seemed to agree with that point of view," Josh said. "He'd expect us to run errands for him. He'd yell at crew members that tried to talk to him. The only people he was nice to were the women, but it came across a little creepy."

"Creepy how? Anything inappropriate? Groping? Or worse?" Sam asked.

"Nothing like that. That I know of. But he'd call them baby and darling and sexy thang," Josh replied.

"I get that every day," Sam wisecracked. "How'd the women react?"

Sam glanced in the rear-view mirror. A black Chevy Suburban SUV with tinted windows was behind them. It looked like the SUV that had been parked in Garrett's driveway.

"They just ignored him as best as they could," Josh said. "But I'm sure it pissed them off."

Sam looked back again at the Suburban. It was hanging back, but clearly following them.

"What do you say we take a little detour?" Sam asked.

Before Josh could answer, Sam swung a hard right on to a residential street and picked up speed. He knew he'd be hitting a county road in two blocks. The Suburban turned right as well but stayed back.

"Hang on," Sam said.

Josh noticed Sam looking in the rear-view mirror and turned to see the Suburban.

"Are they following us?" he asked.

"Not for long."

Sam gunned it as he turned left on to the county road, barely evading a semi-truck traveling in the opposite direction. It was just enough of a diversion to give Sam a good head start. He floored it and picked up speed fast. Other than the semi, there was no traffic. But it was a winding road and Sam's truck screeched as it maneuvered each curve.

For a while, it looked as though they had lost the black Suburban and Sam started to relax. But just as he started to lift his foot off the pedal, the SUV emerged.

"What do they want?" Josh asked.

"I don't want to find out," Sam answered.

Luckily, Sam knew this county road well. He also knew several of the back roads that split off of it. Hopefully, the driver of the Suburban wasn't as familiar with them. Sam spotted a dirt road that disappeared into a thicket of pine trees. It was the back way into the land where he had a small fishing cabin, and he knew the main dirt road would branch off into several smaller dirt roads in the woods. Sam pulled the steering wheel hard, almost lifting the truck up on to two wheels. He made the turn and disappeared into the trees.

The Suburban was too big and going too fast to make the turn. It screeched to a halt as it passed the dirt road, then backed up and made the turn. It was just enough time to give Sam the edge he needed. His truck barreled down the dirt road, throwing up clouds of red dust behind him. The dirt was going to give him away. Seeing a clearing just wide enough for his truck, Sam slowed down and turned. He drove carefully, maneuvering over the soft pine needles through the trees. Recognizing landmarks, he drove until he knew he was out of sight of the dirt path. Then he killed the engine and waited.

Josh started to ask what was happening, but Sam put a finger to his lips to quiet him. He reached under his seat and retrieved his Glock 19. Then he listened.

He could hear the Suburban's engine as it traveled the dirt road. Stopping. Backing up and trying a different road. Finally, the engine sounds faded. Sam waited a few minutes to be sure they were gone, then turned the key to his truck's ignition. He backed up slowly through the trees until he wound his way back to the dirt road, then retraced his route to the county road.

"Holy shit, that was cool as hell," Josh said.

"We got lucky," Sam said.

"What do you think they were doing?"

"They didn't shoot at us, and they had the opportunity," Sam said. "And they didn't try to run us off the road or anything. They also didn't seem to hide what they were doing. So, they were either sloppy, or they were trying to intimidate us. Which worked, by the way."

"Really? You looked cool as a cucumber," Josh said.

"I panic on the inside," Sam replied.

He looked out the side window of his truck.

"Hey, isn't that where Decker's body was found?"

"I guess," Josh replied. "These river bottoms all look the same to me."

"Come on," Sam said. "I want to take another look at the crime scene."

14

THE POND WAS QUITE a distance from where Sam had left his truck and Josh was beginning to wonder if Sam was confused. But then he saw the still green water and could make out the clearing on the other side.

"The parking lot is over there, past that field, right?" Sam asked. "I figure the killer isn't gonna want to drag the body all the way over here. So he probably drove through the field to get closer to the pond."

"So there'd be tire tracks," Josh said.

"There would be. Except you all showed up the next morning, driving and walking through the field. Lots of equipment trucks, ATVs...."

"Couple of makeup trailers and generators," Josh added. "We covered up anything that was here before us."

"Exactly," Sam replied.

The sun was dropping low in the late afternoon sky and the trees were casting long, dark shadows into the swamp. Sam and

Josh walked over to where the killer probably parked and began to walk toward the pond.

"Even if he kept his car's headlights on, the pond is completely hidden from up here. That means the killer had to already know it was there," Sam said.

"So you think he was local?" Josh asked.

"Maybe. But all of you knew it was here, too," Sam said. "How much of the cast and crew were out here?"

"Pretty much everyone. I'm sure we prepped the area for a few days before shooting started. And people would have scouted it before then," Josh said. "We're a small crew. Anyone would know about the pond. Everyone would have."

As they stepped into the woods, the tall trees absorbed the sunlight and everything became darker. Sam reached into his pocket and pulled out the small flashlight Carla had given him. He clicked it on and pointed the beam of light ahead of him, spotting the yellow police tape that was still blocking off the area where Decker's leg had been found.

Sam put himself in the mind of the killer. He began talking out loud as he walked the area.

"So, even if the killer wasn't in the film crew, he probably knew about the movie being filmed there. So why here? If they just wanted to dump the body, there are a million better places."

"To send a message?" Josh asked. "Maybe they wanted me to find Decker's body?" Josh asked.

"Maybe," Sam replied. "Or maybe they knew about the alligators and were counting on them to destroy the evidence."

They crawled under the plastic band of police tape to get closer to the water, shining the flashlight to make sure there were no alligators sitting along the pond's edge. Sam stopped suddenly when he realized there was a five foot, steep slope that emptied into the water. He imagined the killer stood at this very spot. It's where he threw the pieces, one by one, out toward the middle of the pond.

Sam went through the process, hoping the exercise would point out something that could help identify a suspect. But the muddy ground was slippery and Sam lost his balance. As Josh watched, Sam fell down the embankment and splashed into the water.

15

SAM STRUGGLED to find something to pull up from. A vine. A root. Anything. But the embankment was nothing but mud. Very slippery mud. He looked down at his leg.

"You alright?" Josh asked.

"I'm fine," Sam growled, more than a little embarrassed.

"You need any help?" Josh asked.

Sam didn't answer. Figuring his best bet would be to move down the pond embankment to a place that wasn't as steep and slippery, Sam began to slowly pull himself along the edge of the water. Under the thick shade of the cypress and weeping willows, it was dark enough that he had trouble making out what was in front of him. And he knew there were enough snakes and gators and other surprises in this pond that he didn't want to sneak up on anything. He started making loud noises and splashes in hopes of spooking away any sleeping surprise. Of course, all the splashing could also draw the attention of an alligator. Still, the terror of being surprised by a water moccasin outweighed the possibility of luring a gator, so Sam splashed the water and shouted at anything in front of him.

"Hey! Hey! Get out! Coming through!"

"You see something?" Josh asked.

"I'm trying not to see something," Sam explained.

He moved slowly, giving any creature time enough to flee. Always pushing forward but ready to jump back at the slightest sound.

Then he heard something moving in the water behind him.

He spun around and tried to make out any movement in the dark. Was it an animal running from the sound? Or an alligator responding to it? There was just enough light for Sam to make out a ripple in the water. He gulped and froze in fear, staring into the darkness at whatever was there.

"Help me get out of here," he yelled up at Josh.

"You can't get out?" Josh asked, somewhat surprised.

"If I could have, I would have by now," Sam said. "It's too slippery. Hurry."

Josh looked around and grabbed hold of an old cypress tree jutting out of the water's edge. He wrapped his arms around it and then extended his leg, so it was within Sam's reach.

"Grab my leg," he said.

"Are you crazy?" Sam asked.

"You got a better idea?"

Sam heard a faint splash again. This time it was closer.

He reached up as far as his arms could stretch and grabbed hold of the cuff of Josh's jeans. He pulled himself up until he was able to grab Josh's ankle.

"Don't pull me down with you," Josh said.

"Just hang on to the damn tree."

Josh summoned all of his strength to bend his leg, pulling Sam up.

"You're heavier than you look," Josh grunted.

"My clothes are wet," Sam replied.

Sam felt his body being lifted out of the water and he looked around for something more stable to grab. As soon as he spotted some exposed roots of the cypress tree, he grabbed hold and let go of Josh's leg. Josh turned and laid on his stomach, reaching down to help Sam up.

Sam climbed frantically, trying to lift his legs as far away from the water as possible. He grabbed hold of Josh's hand and the two of them worked together to pull Sam up on solid land.

Sam spun around to further distance himself from the water's edge. He crawled backwards and Josh helped him stand.

"You're soaked," Josh said.

But Sam didn't answer. His concentration was fixed on the water and the approaching menace. He heard another small splash, this time right next to where he had been. And then he saw it.

Two brown and black ducks.

Sam's heart fell into his knees and took a breath for what seemed like the first time.

16

SAM AND JOSH walked into the kitchen to find Carla was staring into the freezer.

"Looking for penguins?" he asked with a wink.

Carla stared ahead, not realizing she had a guest. "Looking for dinner."

"Make sure you find something that's enough for three," Sam said.

Carla looked up to see Josh and Sam looking at her. She slammed the freezer door shut, as if to hide the fact that she was looking for dinner.

"Sam, you should have told me we'd be having company," she said through a smile.

"I'm sorry," Josh said. "I don't want to be an imposition. Sam insisted."

"No, no, no," Carla said. "It's no problem. I would have just gone to the store to get something special."

"I don't want to be a bother at all," Josh said.

"It's no bother," Sam said before turning to Carla. "I warned him we tend to order out or microwave in."

"In that case," Carla said, opening the freezer door again and pulling out a large box. "You like lasagna?"

WHILE THE FROZEN LASAGNA COOKED, Josh reveled in telling Carla about Sam's near brush with death in the pond.

"He was terrified," Josh said, laughing.

"I was not," Sam said. "But you would have been, too. You saw what those alligators can do."

"So did you arrest them?" Carla asked. "Did they have anything to do with Decker's death?"

"The feared East Texas Piranha Ducks," Josh replied. "Why aren't we making a movie about them?"

"Are you both enjoying yourself?" Sam asked. "Having fun?"

Carla kissed Sam on the forehead.

"I know you're not afraid of ducks," she said, before turning to Josh, trying to keep a straight face. "But butterflies? That's a different story."

Carla and Josh burst out laughing. Sam finally gave in and laughed along with them. When they finally settled down, Josh tried to make up for the teasing.

"You did take me on a pretty bad ass car chase," he said.

"That was barely a chase," Sam replied. "More like me trying to get away from someone following me."

"Babe, that is the literal definition of a chase," Carla teased.

"Yeah, but they weren't really chasing us," Sam continued.

"Just tailing us. The only thing that made it dramatic was me taking a sharp left corner to try and shake him."

"Don't forget about cutting off the road in the woods," Josh added. "Losing him by out-thinking him, not out-running him. It was bad-ass. And really? You're going to go all humble now? I'm throwing you a bone here, Lawson."

You're right. It was bad ass," Sam said, puffing up with false pride. "I can hide with the best of them."

"Who was it?" Carla asked.

"My money's on one of Garrett's men," Sam said. "But it could have been crazy Josh Cole fans, for all I know. Which, by the way, Garrett is one of."

"The man has good taste," Carla said, smiling at their guest.

Sam opened his mouth in mock shock.

"I am in the room," he said. "Literally, right next to you."

Carla giggled and leaned over to give Sam a kiss.

"I'm glad you're alright," she said. "Both of you."

THIRTY MINUTES LATER, the three of them sat down at the small round table in the kitchen.

"I'm so embarrassed that dinner came frozen in a box," Carla said. She hadn't stopped apologizing since Josh arrived.

"I assure you, it's still better than most of the food I've been having," Josh replied.

"Still, had I known, I could have prepared a nice southern meal for you."

She glanced at Sam who was looking at her in shock.

"Well, I would have picked something up from a nice restaurant," she corrected.

"Carla has a billion strengths. Cooking ain't one of them."

"I could cook if I wanted to," Carla replied. "I just don't like it. I slave over cold bodies all day long. The last thing I want to do is come home and slice more things up."

Sam looked down at his lasagna in a different light and felt a small wave of nausea pass over.

"I promise you. There is nothing to apologize for," Josh said. "It's more about the company anyway."

He raised his glass of wine to Carla and she clinked it with her own. Sam fumbled to grab his beer bottle and join in the toast.

"So, I know you're from East Texas," Carla said. "But what part?"

"South of here," he replied. "Just north of Beaumont."

"How'd you get from Beaumont to Hollywood?" Sam asked.

"A broken heart," Josh replied with a smirk. "Her name was Shelley. Most beautiful girl you'd ever seen. We were young and in love and on top of the world. Or at least I thought we were. Until she told me she didn't love me anymore."

"That's a tell-tell clue," Sam said. He started to laugh at his own joke, but Carla's scolding glance silenced him.

"You know how it is," Josh continued. "Small town. You can't go anywhere without seeing each other. Then she started dating someone else and that was just too much. So I packed a bag and got the hell out of town. I liked doing plays in high school so, on a whim, I moved to LA to become an actor. I figured if it didn't work out, I could at least learn how to surf."

"And the rest is history," Sam said.

"Well, I did a lot of surfing for about ten years," Josh laughed. "But eventually I got a break."

"Have you seen her since?" Carla asked.

Josh laughed and shook his head.

"Shelley? No. And to be honest, I still don't know if I could handle it. And I do realize how pathetic that sounds."

"I think it's romantic," Carla replied.

"Oh, not like that," Josh said. "We've both moved on. We were just kids. Now she's married. Couple of kids. But she still haunts me. Although, to be honest, it's probably just pride at this point. The one that got away."

"Well, now you have women falling at your feet every day," Sam said. "That's some sweet revenge."

"I actually don't date much," Josh said. "LA is weird. I just stay focused on my work."

"May I remind you that your work involves pretending to have sex with beautiful women?" Sam teased.

Josh laughed.

"I ain't gonna lie. It's a weird life, but it ain't a bad one. I'm just ready to do something different. Like this movie. It's a departure for me. Could open up a lot of doors."

"Bigfoot romances?" Sam asked.

17

AFTER DINNER, Sam drove Josh back to the hotel and returned to find Carla sitting on the couch watching TV.

"Please tell me you're not watching one of his movies," Sam said.

Carla grabbed the remote and turned off the TV before Sam could see what she was watching.

"Just flipping through the channels, waiting for you."

Sam plopped down next to her on the couch.

"By the way, Mr. Movie Star is no longer allowed in the morgue," Sam said. "Or anywhere near you."

"Oh, come on," Carla said. "Why do you get to have all the fun? You spent at least part of your day staring at young actresses in bikinis."

Sam started to ask how she knew, but Carla answered before he could.

"I know everything, Sam Lawson. Don't you forget it."

She kissed him on the forehead then playfully patted his cheek.

"So, does Garrett look like our killer?" she asked, switching subjects.

"He sure doesn't look innocent. Unfortunately, he appears to have a choice of solid alibis, so we'll need to build a solid case."

"He probably wouldn't get his own hands dirty, would he? He probably had one of his goons do the deed."

"Yeah. Ramirez is checking all of their alibis now. At least the goons we know of."

Sam scooted closer to Carla and put an arm around her. She nestled in, resting her head on his chest.

"But Garrett made a good point," Sam said. "If Decker owed him money, it wouldn't serve any purpose to kill him."

"Unless Decker couldn't come up with the money," Carla said.

"He ran a string of strip clubs. In one weekend, he could skim enough money to cover any debt," Sam replied.

"Maybe he just refused to pay."

Sam nodded, considering that possibility.

"He seemed to be just arrogant enough to do that. The man was a real dick. Tomorrow I'm going to talk to more of the film crew."

"The ones in bikinis?" Carla asked.

"Let's hope so."

Carla elbowed Sam in the ribs.

"Nothing personal, but no one's even going to notice you with a guy like Josh Cole standing beside you," Carla teased.

"Gee, thanks honey."

"Tell you what. You bring Josh by the morgue and I'll keep an eye on him while you interview your bikini friends."

"I told you. He is not allowed near you," Sam said, pulling Carla's face to his so he could kiss her.

"So how was it?" she asked between kisses. "Babysitting Mr. Romance Movie Star?"

She climbed on top of him and Sam groaned in approval.

"That puppy dog? He spent most of the day trying to impress me. It was kinda cute, actually."

"Mmm-hmm," Carla said, kissing Sam's neck. "I'm sure that's exactly what happened."

"Hey. I'll have you know I'm very impressive."

Carla kissed Sam on the lips. Gently at first, then more passionately.

"Oh, yes. You're very, very impressive."

Sam kissed her back but then pulled back.

"You're not thinking about him right now, are you?"

"Would you stop talking?" Carla said as she pulled him on top of her. "You're ruining my concentration."

18

JASMINE SLOWLY WOKE up to the feeling she was submerged in dark water. While she wasn't able to breathe, she somehow seemed to get air. The water felt thick and heavy around her, making it hard to move. As her body slogged back and forth in the thick liquid, she slowly became aware that she couldn't feel her arms. She struggled to see and was finally able to make out the shape of something in front of her. Then, without warning, Jasmine felt her body being yanked upward by her arms. As her body raced through the water toward the surface, a feeling of panic began to overwhelm her.

She awoke from the nightmare with a heavy gasp, except now she was very aware of not being able to breathe well. As the dream ran off her mind, an ache in her shoulders became increasingly apparent. She slowly realized that her arms were over her head and she was hanging below them. As she struggled to breathe, she became aware of something in her mouth. She struggled to free herself.

Was this still a dream? A worse dream?

She pulled herself out of the fog and quickly realized she had awakened to a nightmare.

Her hands were bound over her head and she tried to shake herself free. That's when she realized she was dangling in the air. Her feet weren't touching the ground. When she tried to scream she realized she had been gagged.

She glanced around, trying to take in her surroundings. But the room was dark and all she could make out was a mass about four feet in front of her.

"Oh, good," the mass purred in a deep, gravely voice. "You're awake."

A bright light exploded in front of her as the mass seemed to turn on an electric lamp.

"I didn't want the light to hit you all at once," the mass said. "But now that you're up..."

Jasmine's eyes adjusted to the light. She was in a small room. Wood walls. Like a work shed. A moldy, earthy, rotten egg smell began to overwhelm her.

I'm in the swamp, she thought.

The mass in front of her began to morph into a large, older man. He was grinning widely at her.

"Hello, slut," he said.

He stepped toward her and Jasmine struggled in vain.

He shushed her.

"Just be still," he said in a soothing voice.

He ran a hand down one of her cheeks. She could feel the coarse, dry skin and the smell of antiseptic.

"Let's take a look here," he said, pushing her black hair away from her ears. "Oh, these are nice."

He carefully removed a gold starfish earring.

"You like starfish?" he asked. "Did you know starfish don't

have any blood? When you cut them, they don't bleed. Such a shame. I like blood."

Tears streamed down Jasmine's cheek and into the cloth gag tied around her mouth.

Ken Mullen took the earring and placed it in a small box on the table behind him.

"I'll take good care of this," he said. "I promise."

He grabbed another earring from a different box and held it up for Jasmine to see. It was a blue gemstone set in a gold mount.

"Isn't this pretty?" he asked. "I don't know what it's called. Do you?"

He caressed her cheek with the earring before inserting it in her naked ear.

"This is actually a bit premature for my liking," he said while putting in the earring. "But you know what they say the key is to a long life? Being able to adapt."

He stood back to look at the earring in Jasmine's ear.

"That's nice," he said.

He turned his back to Jasmine, opening up a leather bag on the table.

"You know, you really should feel honored," he said. "Your death is going to serve a much higher purpose."

Jasmine watched in horror as he unrolled the leather bag, revealing several large knives. She screamed through the gag but the cloth muffled the sound.

"Oh, hush," Mullen said, turning around with a large syringe. "We're only just beginning to have fun."

Jasmine felt the sting of the needle as it pierced her neck. In seconds, she felt herself sinking back into unconsciousness.

19

BRIAN AND MATT crouched down in the cavern, taking in the detail of the rocks that surrounded them. Their heads bobbed to the Grateful Dead song jamming from the small speaker of one of their phones.

"A little more over here," Matt said, pointing to an unpainted section of rock.

Brian dipped the paintbrush in the bucket next to him and touched up the fiberglass rock.

Brian and Matt were set decorators and, because of the shift in shooting schedule because of Decker's death, they had been tasked with the arduous task of preparing all the fake caverns in a day. Now late at night, they were the only two still in the movie warehouse, so they took advantage of the privacy by lighting up a joint as they painted.

Matt, in his late thirties, was the older of the two by a few years. He was chunky with a pompadour haircut that somehow always managed to stay in place, even in the Texas heat and humidity. He took a drag on the joint and watched his partner paint then rewarded Brian's work by passing the joint to him.

"Looking more and more like a real cave, my man," Matt said.

"It looks like the Batcave," Brian muttered. "This doesn't look real at all."

"Relax. A little lighting, the right camera lens, and we are spelunking, my friend."

Brian laughed.

"You are so stoned," he said.

"Or am I just enlightened?" Matt asked with false seriousness.

They both laughed quietly but were distracted by a very different sound. An angry woman was yelling.

The two climbed through the fake tunnel toward the noise. The side warehouse garage door that opened to the office trailers was still open and the silhouette of a woman could be seen pointing and yelling.

Brian turned down the speaker on his phone and the Dead faded until they could hear the woman. They weren't able to make out what she was saying, but it was clear she was pissed. They craned their necks to see if they could see the object of her fury but, whoever they were, they were just out of sight.

As the woman yelled, the two men were able to pick out stray phrases.

"You owe me."

"You better be afraid of me."

"You don't want me on your bad side."

The woman finally stopped yelling and stormed away. Brian and Matt shrunk back into the shadows of the cave so they couldn't be seen. The woman, unaware of the two stoned voyeurs, stomped past them toward the door. The work lights aimed at the caverns splashed across her face. It was a very pissed off Chloe Bernard.

20

THE NEXT MORNING, Sam headed straight to the movie set. He hoped to speak to a few members of the cast and crew without his new trusty sidekick. Not that Josh was that much of a nuisance, but Sam was used to working alone. And he figured the movie people might be more forthcoming if one of their own wasn't doing the questioning.

He arrived at the warehouse around nine, figuring these Hollywood types partied all night and didn't start working until later in the day. He was surprised to find the warehouse buzzing with all sorts of people. Very busy, hard-working people. Some were hauling bags of sand toward the set, others were laying out cable and other electrical equipment. A young woman with purple hair and a nose ring was barking out orders into the microphone of her headset. He figured she might be a good person to start with but before he could approach her, she called someone's name and rushed off in a different direction.

Not sure where to go first, Sam turned and ran into a wall of matted, smelly fur. He stepped back to see a giant Bigfoot creature snarling down at him.

"Sorry, sir," came a shy voice from inside the suit. "It's hard to see in this thing."

Sam nodded and stepped aside, watching the monster lope toward the cave set.

"Pretty rad, right?" another voice asked.

Sam turned to see Chad McGinnis. The director was watching Bigfoot with admiration.

"We went through seventeen iterations before we came up with that look," he said. "I think we nailed it."

"Mr. McGinnis," Sam said.

"Who's that?" Chad said. "Call me Chad. I ain't my dad."

He laughed at his stupid rhyme. Sam did not.

"Do you have a second? I need to ask you a few more questions about Vince Decker."

Chad looked toward the cave set.

"We're about to shoot," he said as he started walking to the set. "Come watch. You'll dig it."

Since he was no longer a cop, Sam didn't have the authority to make Chad talk to him. Besides, it would be cool to watch them film something. He tagged along behind the director.

"You just have to be quiet," Chad instructed. "And no pictures."

Sam started toward a large cave set with a dirt floor. He was surprised when Chad started walking away from the set toward a wall of television monitors. The monitors formed a wall that blocked the actual set. A row of director's chairs sat on the other side, facing the monitors.

"Welcome to our Video Village," Chad said, sitting down in

one of the chairs. An assistant gave him a clipboard and he read it while studying the image on the screens. It was the cavern set that was literally on the other side of the monitors. Sam looked at the live set then at the monitors and was amazed at the difference. The actual set looked fake and small, but on the monitor it looked eerie and like it went on forever.

An assistant motioned Sam toward one of the director's chairs and the detective sat down, mesmerized by his surroundings. He craned his neck to see three Bigfoot characters sitting in folding chairs and sucking Big Gulps through giant straws.

"They're local high school kids," the assistant said. "Tallest basketball players we could find in the county."

Sam suddenly had a million questions but before he could ask anything, he was interrupted by the booming voice of a tall red-headed man with a movie clapboard.

"Quiet on the set! Scene 56. Take 8."

"Sound!" yelled another man seated next to a machine and wearing a large pair of headphones.

Sam was suddenly aware of a cameraman standing on the other side of the monitors, he was seated low on a small chair with rollers attached to a set of tracks. Another man stood just off the stage holding a large boom mic in the air.

"Annnnnd ACTION!" Chad yelled.

Sam saw the movement on the monitor before he saw it in real life. A giant Bigfoot character was grunting as he dragged something behind him. It was a woman and she was shrieking in terror as he dragged her by her hair into the main cavern and against the wall. The woman was the brunette actress that Sam had met by the pool. Ana something. She was covered in blood and bruises and her clothes were ripped so they barely covered her.

She looked up at her Bigfoot captor and let out a bloodcurdling scream. The Bigfoot yelled back. And it sounded like a teenage boy trying to yell. It was anything but scary.

"Cut!" Chad yelled, as he jumped out of his chair.

He looked at the stunned look on Sam's face.

"We'll put in a good animal roar later," he said with a wink.

"That was great guys," he said enthusiastically to his actors as he walked toward the set.

"This asshole is ripping my hair out of my head," Ana yelled.

"I'm sorry, Miss Ford," a teenage voice squeaked from inside the giant Bigfoot suit. "It's hard to tell what I'm grabbing in this thing."

"Well, here's a tip for you. If I start screaming, you've grabbed wrong," Ana yelled back.

"I'm sure Tyler here just thought you were acting," Chad interjected. "Right, Tyler?"

"It's Taylor," the Bigfoot corrected.

"I refuse to do this again," Ana said. "I bet my scalp is bleeding."

She turned and lifted up her hair. An assistant rushed over but Chad shooed her away.

"Let me take a look," he said calmly.

He half-glanced at her hair.

"It's fine," he said. "A little pink but nothing bad."

"Either way, we're done with this scene," she said, before storming off.

The dejected Bigfoot raised his hands in frustration.

"I said I was sorry."

"It's okay," Chad said loudly. "We got what we need. This scene is a wrap. Let's move on to the next."

Chad walked back behind the monitors and whispered in hush tones with one of his assistants as they looked over a script. The assistant scurried off and Chad turned to Sam.

"Pretty wild, huh?" he asked. "I mean, it wasn't that big of a scene, but still."

"It was amazing," Sam said. "All that trouble for a little tiny moment."

"That's all movies are, man. Just a lot of small moments put together. And then a few big kick-ass moments, too," Chad said with a big grin. "Now what did you need? You've got five minutes. If I start running behind this early in the day, it will throw everything off."

Sam asked Chad the questions he was unable to ask when they last met. If Decker had any enemies. If he had mentioned anything about anyone. He also repeated some of the questions he had already asked—to see if Chad's answers changed. But the director shrugged off each question.

"You ever see him in Fox 2000?" Chad asked. "The guy was a powerhouse. Not so much anymore, but it took a lot of ass-kissing to get him to come on board this movie. And now I've got to find some other has-been."

"I'm sorry for your loss," Sam said.

"Hey, I'm not a heartless bastard. I feel bad he's dead and all. But it's not like he left a grieving wife and family behind. Can we be honest? No one liked him. But his being a jerk fit the dynamic. Created tension I could use. You know what I mean?"

"Absolutely," Sam said. "What good is an asshole if you can't use it?"

Chad grinned and nodded, mistaking Sam's sarcasm for wisdom.

"Yeah. You get it."

He patted Sam on the shoulder a little too hard.

"Look. You're welcome to hang around and talk to anyone you want. Just respect the quiet when we're rolling. And try not to interfere with my actors too much. They need to stay in character. Speaking of which..."

Sam turned in the direction of Chad's gaze to see Josh sauntering toward them. He grinned and winked at Sam.

"Josh. You're not on the call sheet today," Chad said.

"I was looking for this guy," Josh said, nodding toward Sam. "Your lovely fiancé told me you'd be here."

"You talked to Carla?" Sam asked, fighting a jolt of jealousy.

"I figured who else would know best where to find you."

Chad excused himself and walked toward the set. Josh looked around the set, taking it all in.

"I love movie sets," he said. "There ain't nothing else like it. I mean, look at all of these people. Salt of the earth electricians and construction workers as well as painters and actors. Tradesmen and artists all working together. Like a big factory with one mission: bringing a dream to life."

Sam looked at Josh.

"You practiced that, didn't you?" Sam asked.

"Been rehearsing for days," Josh replied with a wink.

Sam laughed.

"What are you doing here anyway?" Sam asked.

Josh turned and saluted Sam.

"Reporting for duty, sir," he said. "What adventures do you have planned for me today?"

"You're going to find this hard to believe, but none of what I do is planned for you," Sam said. "And there's not a lot of adventure to this morning. Just asking people what they know about Decker."

Sam spotted the writer who had stormed out of Guzman's office the day before. He was standing over a table covered in pastries and fruit, no doubt struggling between choosing healthy or delicious.

"And I just found who I need to talk to next."

21

JOSH AND SAM walked over to where Richard Fowler was pouring a cup of coffee. Now able to get a better look at Fowler, Sam was surprised by his square jaw and muscular body that seemed more befitting of an actor.

"Hey, Richard," Josh said. "Want you to meet Sam Lawson. He's a real PI working the murder. I'm tagging along to help me develop my character."

"Or you could take your inspiration from what's in the script," Fowler remarked.

Josh nodded in an effort to appease the writer's ego. Fowler accepted the unspoken treaty and turned to Sam.

"So, you're working Vince Decker's murder, huh?"

"You don't seem surprised he was killed," Sam said.

"It makes sense."

"How does it make sense?" Sam asked.

"Between the business he was in to just being a total asshole, he was bound to have enemies in all the wrong places," Fowler said. "I was shocked, but not surprised."

"Would you mind if I ask you a few questions?" Sam asked.

Fowler shrugged. "I already talked to the police, but sure."

He motioned at a few director's chairs and the three sat down. Fowler surveyed the set.

"All here bringing my words to life. It's humbling," he said with absolutely no humility.

He took a sip of coffee and winced.

"So, how's the shadowing going?" Fowler asked Josh.

"I've already rubbed shoulders with a drug kingpin and got caught in a car chase," Josh bragged. "And that was just Day One."

"You started off hot," Sam chuckled. "Trust me. It's not normally that action-packed."

"How long have you been a P.I.?" Fowler asked.

"Just a few months," Sam answered. "Was a cop before that."

"What made you jump ship?" Fowler asked.

"Aren't I the one that's supposed to be asking the questions?" Sam asked with a smirk.

Fowler raised his hands. "Sorry. Occupational habit," he said. "Or just an annoying habit. Depends on who you ask."

Sam asked Fowler the usual questions. About his relationship with Decker. If he had noticed anything suspicious or anyone suspicious hanging around.

"I'll tell you the same thing I told the police," Fowler said. "Decker and I didn't like each other, but we're both professionals. We stayed civil. Any flare-ups we had were all part of the process. Hashing out creative differences. Perfectly normal."

He looked at Josh to back him up. The actor nodded.

"More normal than not," Josh said.

"To be honest, I was grateful for him. If it wasn't for his involvement, and his investment, this film wouldn't be getting made."

"Did you notice anything odd?" Sam asked. "Anyone hanging around that was out of the ordinary?"

"Anyone suspicious hanging around? That's hard to say," Fowler said. "There are always onlookers and gawkers. And, to me, they all look suspicious. But that's my writer's brain. Overactive imagination."

Sam could practically feel the pretentiousness dripping off the words.

"You mind telling us where you were between 2 and 3 a.m. Sunday morning?" Josh asked.

The fact that Josh asked the question surprised both Sam and Fowler.

"Did I say it wrong?" Josh asked Sam.

Sam started to admonish Josh for overstepping his bounds, but Fowler spoke first.

"That was good," he said. "Sounded real. And, since it's the obvious question you're going to ask me anyway, I'll tell you that I was sleeping soundly in my room, unlike most of these carnies."

He motioned at the crew members working throughout the warehouse.

"I've asked to be moved several times," Fowler complained. "There's no way every room in that hotel is occupied."

"Parties?" Sam asked.

"There's always a party," Josh said with a laugh.

"Was there a party Saturday night?" Sam asked Fowler.

"Room 227," Fowler answered. "I walked past the open door

on the way to my room and I knew it was going to be another long night."

"What time was that?" Sam asked.

"I don't know. 10? 11?"

"We need to find out who is in Room 227," Sam said to Josh.

"Oh, I already know," Josh said. "I was there."

22

THE THREE MEN were interrupted by the arrival of Detective Ramirez.

"Oh, look," Ramirez said. "It's not-a-police-officer-anymore Sam Lawson."

"Ramirez," Sam said, ignoring the comment. "You saved me a phone call. Got some new information for you."

"Can I be excused?" Fowler asked. "I need to talk to Guzman about the script. If he wants more rewrites, I want more money."

"Just don't leave the area," Ramirez said.

"So, did you know there was a party the night of the murder?" Sam asked Ramirez before turning to Josh. "Was Decker there?"

"I didn't see him," Josh shrugged. "But I wasn't there that long."

Ramirez raised a hand to slow Sam down.

"You don't think we haven't already interviewed the entire

cast and crew?" Ramirez asked. "I already know about the party. And who was there."

"So was Decker there?" Sam asked.

"No one remembers," Ramirez muttered. "But the hotel has records of what time people use their key cards to come and go, so we'll be able to construct a pretty good timetable."

Josh laughed.

"That's not gonna tell you anything," he said. "We have the whole hotel, so everyone props their doors open. Or puts a piece of paper in the door so it doesn't lock. That way we don't have to carry our keycard around with us."

Ramirez let out a sigh.

"Everyone does it?" he asked.

"Everyone I know of," Josh said with a shrug. "But, listen. If you want to know who was at the party, why not talk to the host?"

He patted Ramirez on the back and turned him toward a tall, skinny man with shoulder-length salt-and-pepper hair.

"Hey, Ben!" Josh yelled out.

Ben Tiernon turned toward them and Josh waved him over.

"Ben," said Josh. "This is Detective Ramirez and Sam Lawson."

"He is NOT a detective," Ramirez added, motioning to Sam.

"I'm a PRIVATE detective," Sam corrected.

Ben smiled. It was a beaming, friendly smile that made him immediately approachable.

"I remember you," Ben said to Ramirez. "Got any leads yet?"

"Ben is our production designer and location scout," Josh said to Sam. "He either finds where we shoot or he builds it."

"So it's your fault all of these people have to deal with East Texas heat and humidity," Sam said. "I bet they hate you."

"Probably," Ben replied, still smiling. "But it's too good an area to pass up. I came here once about ten years ago and never forgot it."

"We were wondering if you could tell us a little more about your party the other night," Josh said.

Ben seemed confused that Josh was leading the conversation.

"Oh. I'm helping them out with the murder case," Josh said.

"No," Sam corrected. "You're shadowing me. As in, standing behind me. In the shadows."

"What else does the shadow want to know?" Ben asked Josh.

"Just a few more questions, if you don't mind," Sam said, trying to steer the conversation back to him. "Like, what time did the party start?"

"That's a good question," Ben answered with a laugh. "On weekends, the hotel is like Vegas. Time starts to blur. Know what I mean? We were all hanging at the pool until the hotel finally kicked us out."

"What time was that?" Ramirez asked.

Ben shrugged. "I couldn't tell you. Ten? Eleven?"

"And then you all just went up to your room?" Sam asked.

Ben nodded.

"I already had a lot of booze in the room from the night before."

"So, you throw a lot of parties?" Ramirez asked.

Josh and Ben both laughed.

"Don't get me wrong. When we're shooting, we're total professionals. Most of us have to be on set at the crack of dawn so we go to bed early. And they are long-ass days. So, when we get a break, we like to blow off steam."

"So, you had a party both Friday and Saturday night," Ramirez said.

"Yeah," Ben said. "And your shadow buddy here is a crazy man, by the way."

"Vince Decker ever come to your parties?" Sam asked.

Ben shook his head.

"I invited him once," Ben said. "He acted like he was too good for us."

"What about Saturday night?" Ramirez asked. "Did you invite him then?"

"Why bother?"

"Did you see him at all Saturday night?" Sam asked.

Ben shrugged.

"I saw him late afternoon. I cut through the lobby to go to the men's room," Ben said. "He was in a hallway talking to Chad."

"The director?" Sam asked.

Ben nodded. "Yeah. They were acting all shifty. Looked like Chad was giving Decker something, like a good old-fashioned drug exchange."

"Wait," Ramirez interrupted. "Chad was buying drugs from Decker?"

Ben shrugged. "I said it looked like it. I don't know what went down. But when I came back out of the bathroom, they were still there. Having a pretty intense conversation. All whispers and shit, you know?"

"So, you didn't hear anything?" Sam asked.

Ben shook his head. "I didn't try. Was none of my business. I just headed back to the pool. Look. I gotta get to set."

Ramirez nodded and Ben flashed another big grin before walking off.

"Guess I need to talk to Chad," Ramirez said.

"I just did," Sam said. "And he's on set right now so, good luck with that."

Ramirez pulled out his badge.

"He doesn't have to talk to you," Ramirez said. "He doesn't have a choice with me."

"Fine. Let's go."

"I said, I need to talk to Chad," Ramirez corrected.

"Why do you get to question him alone?" Sam asked.

"Because I'm the cop," Ramirez said. "I can bring Chad McGinnis into the station and interrogate him properly. On my turf, not here."

"Well, what the hell am I supposed to do?" Sam asked.

"I don't know," Ramirez said. "Go do private detective stuff."

Sam watched helplessly as Ramirez left them. He turned to Josh.

"Who else can we talk to?" Sam asked. "I already hit up the director and the writer."

Josh laughed.

"You're doing this all wrong. Those guys don't know shit. But I know who does."

23

JOSH LED Sam back to a side room that had been built in the warehouse. It was brightly lit with a row of chairs, each chair facing a makeup station and large mirror. A young woman in denim shorts and a pink half shirt was cleaning up a few of the desks.

"Hey, Mischa," Josh purred in a flirty drawl.

Her full lips spread into a wide smile, causing her nose to crinkle in the most adorable way. She was one of those people that was instantly likable, and Sam couldn't help but smile as well.

"Hey, Josh," the woman said. "What's up?"

"Mischa, meet Sam Lawton, private eye," Josh said with relish.

Mischa directed her smile towards Sam.

"Nice to meet you, Sam Lawson, private eye."

"Mischa's in the Hair and Makeup department," Josh explained. "Which means she knows everything about everyone."

Of course, thought Sam. *Go to the hair stylist. They always have all the gossip.*

Sam asked her what she knew about Decker. If he had any enemies. If anyone had a reason to kill him.

"I don't like to talk bad about anyone," Mischa said. "Everyone's got their story, right? But Vince didn't fit in. And didn't try to. Because of that, he wasn't very well liked. But I don't think anyone in our crew would kill him. Every once in a while, we get a diva, but we deal. We're used to it. And we all knew he was only going to be on set a few days anyway."

"Did anyone say anything odd or weird?" Sam asked. "Even if you don't think it matters, it could."

"Well, there was one thing that was kind of bizarre," she said. "But it wasn't really a bad thing."

She hesitated and looked at Josh.

"It's okay," Josh said. "He'll keep your name out of it."

"I'll try," Sam added.

Mischa shrugged.

"You know Ana, right?"

She was talking more to Josh than Sam, probably because it felt more like she was talking to a friend than divulging secrets to a stranger.

"I'm pretty sure she and Vince kind of had a thing going."

Josh burst out laughing.

"Ana? Are you shitting me?"

Mischa smiled and shrugged again.

"To each his own, right?" she said. "Maybe she saw something we didn't. Love is love."

Josh laughed, not quite buying Mischa's romantic take on the affair.

"Who's Ana?" Sam asked.

"You met her yesterday," Josh said. "The brunette by the pool."

Sam remembered her well but was having a hard time seeing her with Decker.

"Is she here?" Sam asked.

"She doesn't have any scenes today," Mischa said.

"So, she's probably at the hotel," Josh said.

"Well," Sam said. "Let's go pay Ana a little visit."

24

ANA FORD SAT on the edge of the bed in her hotel room, visibly upset at her unexpected guests.

"You could have at least called in advance," Ana huffed. "I just got out of the shower."

She was patting her wet hair with a towel but had already put on her makeup and was dressed in black leggings and a tight tank top.

"Sorry," Sam said. "We happened to be in the neighborhood."

"I've already given my statement to the police," she said. "Couldn't you just read it?"

"I know. And I apologize. But I'm working for the movie, not the police, so I kind of have to do my thing separately."

"That doesn't seem very efficient," Ana said.

Sam nodded, but before he could ask a question, there was a knock at the door. Josh opened it to Chloe Bernard, who seemed genuinely surprised to see him.

"Josh? What are you doing..."

Before she could finish her sentence, she noticed Sam and pushed past Josh into the room.

"Is everything okay?" she asked. "Ana, what's going on?"

"I just had a few questions for Ana," Sam said. "No big deal."

"And I'd like to hurry this up," Ana said.

"I thought you were done shooting for the day," Josh teased.

"So?" Ana replied. "I need to work out, then tape a video audition. Then I have a meeting with my publicist and then exercises with my dialect coach."

Sam thought it was odd that she showered before working out, but then remembered she had to wash off all the fake flood and bruises that she had been wearing earlier. Even the most hardcore gyms would probably frown on that. He also noticed this stressed-out version of Ana was a far cry from the sultry, flirty woman he had met at the pool just one day earlier. Then again, he had intruded on her day.

"This will just take a minute," Sam said. "I want to know about your interactions with Vince Decker. Like... romantic interactions."

"He flirted with both of us," Chloe said, even though Sam's question was directed at Ana. "It was non-stop. And annoying."

"Ana, what can you tell me about your relationship with Decker," Sam asked.

"I don't know what you mean."

"There was nothing going on between the two of you?" Sam asked.

Ana hesitated and started to answer, but Chloe spoke first.

"I saw him coming to your room."

Ana glared at Chloe and then looked back to Sam and Josh, trying to figure out what to say. She shook her head, prepared to deny it. But then she let out a sigh and dropped her head in surrender.

"Fine," she said. "He came to my room a few times. We're both adults."

"Some more than others," Josh quipped.

"We were running lines," Ana explained.

"Just running lines?" Sam asked.

"That's it. I swear."

Sam could tell Ana was lying.

"Ana. I'm going to find out the truth one way or another," he said. "You should do yourself a favor and tell me now."

"Okay. Fine. It got... intimate," Ana said. "But it was just a little fling. A DISCREET production fling."

She looked at Sam.

"You can't let this get out. We signed NDAs!"

"Well, I didn't. But I'll do what I can if you cooperate," Sam said. "Did you see him Saturday night?"

"No," Ana answered quickly.

"That's not true," Chloe said. "I heard him knocking on your door."

"What time was this?" Sam asked.

"Eleven? Eleven thirty?" Chloe guessed.

"Jesus, Chloe. Are you spying on me?" Ana snapped. "Yeah. He came to my room around eleven. But he didn't stay more than five minutes. He was drunk and I made him leave. Did you hear that, too, Ms. Nosy?"

Chloe shook her head.

"Maybe. I don't know."

"Did he seem upset?" Sam asked.

Ana nodded. "Oh, yeah. He was pissed about something. He just kept mumbling nonsense."

"What did he say?" Sam asked. "Try to remember."

"I don't know," Ana thought. "Something about 'needing it now'."

"Needing what now?" Sam asked.

Ana looked at Sam, waiting for him to figure it out. Sam finally nodded.

"But he didn't get it?" Sam asked.

"I told you," Ana said. "I made him leave."

"Well, if that's true, it will all show up on the security footage," Sam said. "I noticed a camera at the end of the hallway."

"Oh, those are all disabled," Josh said. "Part of the discretionary policy I was telling you about."

"Let's hope the hotel kept the lobby cameras operational," Sam sighed. "Thanks, ladies. I really appreciate your help. I'll let you get on with your day."

"You have to keep this private," Ana said. "If this came out, it would be disastrous for me."

"I don't know," Chloe said. "A little tabloid fodder could be good exposure."

She picked up a pair of tortoise-shell glasses on Ana's dresser.

"I didn't know you wore glasses," she said.

Ana snatched them out of Chloe's hands.

"There's a lot you don't know about me," she snapped.

She looked at the glasses and frowned, as if her secret identity had been revealed. Giving in, she slipped the glasses on and looked at everyone as if she was revealing a major handicap.

"Happy?"

"They look good on you," Josh said.

Ana rolled her eyes and turned her attention back to Sam.

"Please. Promise me you won't go public with this."

"If your story checks out, I'll do what I can to keep it quiet."

He said goodbye and walked out with Josh.

"So, what do you think?" Josh asked. "Ana is the last known person to see him alive."

Sam nodded.

"I don't know. Her story is pretty convenient. But I can have the hotel check when Decker used his key card to get into his room. Or, if he went back out, I'm hoping the hotel security footage will help us."

"For the record, I believe her," Josh said. "Trust me. She's not that good of an actress."

25

DECKER DID NOT SHOW up on the hotel lobby security footage, but Josh quickly pointed out that he likely didn't leave through the front lobby.

"If he parked around back, which he probably did, he probably walked out one of the other exits," Josh said. "That's what I do."

It made perfect sense, but it left Sam with no way to check Ana's story. He decided it was time to explore a different path.

"Are you in any scenes today?" Sam asked.

Josh spread his arms wide.

"I'm all yours."

"You up for a drive to Dallas?"

~

THE MOOD WAS a lot less cordial in Ana's hotel room. Chloe was now sitting on the bed while Ana paced back and forth furiously.

"You couldn't just keep your mouth shut?" she asked.

"I was trying to help you," Chloe said. "If they caught you in a lie, it could've been really bad for you."

"Yeah. You're just looking out for me. Chloe the Girl Scout."

"I wasn't the one sleeping with a dead guy."

Ana put her head in her hands and let out a primal yell.

"This is not happening!"

She glared at Chloe.

"You're really enjoying this, aren't you? You've had it out for me as soon as I was cast. What? Are you threatened?"

"Of you?" Chloe laughed. "Don't flatter yourself. This is my movie. You're just window dressing. Nothing more."

"Don't think I don't know about your secrets," Ana said.

Chloe tried to hide it, but Ana could tell she had hit a nerve.

"I don't know what you're talking about," Chloe said.

Ana bent over so her face was inches from Chloe's.

"Just remember," she seethed. "You fired the first shot. Now get out."

She pointed to the door. Chloe stood, turning to the mirror to check her hair before departing.

"I don't know what you think you know, but if you even try to slander me, I'll bury you so fast you won't even appear in a Google search."

She turned and threw a poisonous smile at Ana.

"Enjoy the rest of your day."

Ana opened the door to let her out and let it slam behind her. She leaned back on the door, letting her tough facade down. Sobbing as she slid to the floor. She had worked so hard to get where she was and now it could all just blow up in her face. She thought about her threat to Chloe. She didn't really know about any secrets but had bet on the fact that everyone had something they didn't want to get out. Regardless, Ana couldn't even think about that right now.

Why did I sleep with him? she asked herself.

It wasn't a power move. Decker didn't have any influence anymore. Maybe she just liked the attention. Or maybe he just literally charmed the pants off of her. He could be charming when he wasn't being an asshole. She made a mental note to talk to her therapist about it. Then she began to shift into problem-solving mode. She needed to get ahead of this. First thing to do would be to call her publicist and come up with a plan in case the affair went public. Maybe Chloe was on to something. The exposure could work in her favor if she could spin it right.

26

THE INTERVIEW with Chad was lasting longer than Ramirez had expected. It was only early afternoon, but the detective felt like he had already worked three days straight. Truth be told, Ramirez hadn't had a good night sleep since Sam quit the force. Even though Chief Bannon had pretty much relegated him to a desk jockey, Sam was always an extra detective when they needed him. And honestly, the fact that he had handled so much of the paperwork had made every detective's job easier.

Chad tapped Ramirez's desk, snapping him back to the present.

"You cost me a half day of filming, but no hard feelings," Chad said. "Everyone's got a job to do. Much respect. Also, do you know where I can get a good iced mocha latte around here?"

"Get out," Ramirez muttered.

Chad put his hands together in prayer and bowed to Ramirez before walking away.

God, I can't wait until this movie leaves town, he thought.

Even before the murder, the movie was spreading the already thin police force even thinner. Between security details, extra patrolling, and traffic control, everyone on the force was pulling double and even triple shifts.

Ramirez grinned, realizing that, for the first time in his life, Sam actually had good timing. He had pulled out right before things went crazy.

He wondered how it was going in Dallas. Ramirez hoped Sam would find something useful in Dallas. As much as he hated having a private detective work the case with him, it was nice having someone else handle a lot of the leg work that took up lots of time with little chance of a payout.

Ramirez pushed back his chair and stood up. He grabbed his coffee cup and headed for the coffee machine, and had just begun to pour some of the brown swill when Bannon called him into his office.

"What's up?" Ramirez asked upon entering the police chief's office.

"I hear tell you're working with Lawson," Bannon snapped.

"Well, he was hired to work the same case so we're combining resources."

"May I remind you that he is no longer a member of this police force? And this murder investigation is a police matter."

"Yes, sir," Ramirez muttered, hoping Bannon would just let it go at that.

"All that said, we may have a problem," Bannon said. "Another sex worker has gone missing."

Ramirez's stomach dropped. That fit Mullen's victimology.

"Do you think?" he started to ask. But Bannon cut him off before he could finish.

"We don't know what it is. Not yet. But we need to treat it like it could be."

Ramirez nodded.

"I'm assigning it to Hicks and Awbrey," Bannon said. "For now. You've got this movie murder case going on. But if it turns into something, I'm gonna need to bring you in. You understand?"

"Yes, sir."

"And Ramirez. I don't think I need to tell you that you can't mutter a word of this to Lawson. Not yet."

"But Chief. He needs to know. Doctor Davenport needs to know. They received a death threat."

"We've already got them under surveillance and Davenport is getting escorted to and from work. We're already doing all we can do there. And this may all be nothing."

"I don't feel right about this," Ramirez said.

"I don't give a rat's ass," Bannon said. "You and I both know girls like this go missing all the time and it's nothing. So we're going to look into it. If anything at all looks fishy, we will let Lawson and Davenport know. But not until then. Got it?"

Ramirez nodded again and began to pray that Hicks and Awbrey found this woman quickly.

27

DOUBLE DIAMONDS GENTLEMEN'S Club was located in Uptown Dallas on a stretch of road populated by several high-end strip clubs. They all had suggestive names like The Cheetah Club, Satin Dolls, and Dreams. At night, pink and purple neon signs lit up the area, drawing lonely businessmen, fraternity brothers and adventurous couples into their seductive web. But in the middle of the afternoon, the area lost most of its luster. Some of the clubs were closed until evening, but a few remained open, hoping to peel some dollar bills away from committed daytime voyeurs.

Sam never really got the allure of strip clubs. All sizzle. No steak. And daytime strip clubs were even more depressing. Josh, on the other hand, was excited about the visit. He saw it as an actor's field trip.

"The place is full of stories," he explained, as they walked in the door. "Why is that guy in the suit here instead of at work? Did that stripper drop her kid off at school before she took her shift? Does she like what she's doing? Does she get a kick out of being the center of attention or does she despise every man that stares at her? It's fascinating!"

"Well, the big question today is 'Why is the owner desperate for money?'" Sam said.

The two looked around the large, dark room. Stage lights bathed everything in a dark red glow. A young brunette danced lazily to a heavy metal power ballad on a small rectangular stage that jutted out of purple curtains along the back wall.

Sam looked around for a manager or even a bartender, but the dancer seemed to be the only person working. She leaned back against a stripper pole, staring straight ahead as she slowly slid her hands over her perfectly round breasts and down to the small piece of red satin between her legs. Three men were spread out in seats along the edge of the stage, lazily waving five- and ten-dollar bills to draw the dancer's attention.

Sam motioned Josh to follow him to the long, chrome bar that ran along one wall, hoping to attract the attention of a hidden bartender. As if on cue, a woman stood up from a table hidden in a shadowy corner. Sam noticed a sandwich and a magazine on the tabletop. They had obviously interrupted her lunch break.

The woman, who looked to be in her mid- to late-thirties, had jet black hair, dark eyeliner and purple lipstick. Her black tank top and leather pants were so tight they looked as if they had been painted on her enhanced body.

"Ten-dollar cover," she yelled over the music, as she lifted a hinged portion of the bar counter and walked behind it.

"We're not here for pleasure," Sam yelled back, instinctively reaching for his badge then remembering he couldn't play that card anymore. "Just need to talk to the manager. About Vince Decker."

The woman looked Sam and Josh up and down.

"Still a ten-dollar cover," she said loudly.

Sam sighed and pulled a twenty out of his wallet. The woman placed it in a plastic pitcher next to the cash register. A different song started blaring through the speakers.

"What about Vince?" she yelled.

Sam was already growing tired of yelling.

"Can we turn that down?" he asked.

The woman looked at him as if he was stupid. Then, letting out a sigh, motioned for Sam to follow her.

"Come back to the office," she yelled. "But only one of you. And don't try anything. There are cameras everywhere and muscle you can't even see."

Sam motioned for Josh to wait.

"Oh, come on," he protested.

"There are worse ways to wait," Sam said with a wink.

The woman turned and walked away, raising her hand and pointing toward the bar. Sam was startled by a large man dressed in black who appeared out of the dark shadows like some sort of hulkish ninja. Sam scanned the room and could make out a couple of other large bodies, standing perfectly still in the shadows, ready to pounce if anything got out of hand.

The large man pulled back the purple curtain, revealing a door. The woman walked toward it and Sam followed, looking back at Josh one last time to see that one of the hidden men had appeared out of nowhere and was standing behind the actor.

~

THE HALLWAY on the other side of the door was dark except for blue track lighting along the floor. Sam guessed it was kept dark so bright lights wouldn't jar everyone into reality every time someone opened the door. The blue glow dead-ended into another door and Sam had to squint from the bright light that hit him when the woman opened it. He was clearly backstage now. Fluorescent lights bounced off a faded white tile floor. To his left was a series of makeup tables and folding chairs that were occupied by young women wearing a lot of makeup and not much else. They looked at Sam curiously and he smiled back at them.

Sam followed the woman through another door into a sparse office with a modest desk pushed up against one wall and two folding chairs next to it. The desk was covered in spreadsheets, paperwork and a laptop. The woman motioned for Sam to sit as she did the same.

"This better?" she asked.

"Thank you," Sam said. "Name's Sam Lawson. I'm a private investigator and I have a few questions about Vince Decker."

"Victoria Perry," the woman said. "I'm the day manager. Who'd the asshole fuck this time?"

She could see Sam was confused.

"The only time anyone hires a private eye is when someone's having an affair," Victoria said.

"Not this time," Sam said. "I'm investigating his murder."

Victoria froze. Stunned.

"Vince is dead?"

Sam offered a brief explanation of Vince's death but painted in broad strokes to avoid leading Victoria down any path before he questioned her.

"You know anyone who would want Vince dead?" Sam asked.

"I don't know," she answered. "He was an asshole and had a lot of enemies, but to kill him?"

"What about his finances?" Sam asked.

"What about them?"

"Did he owe a lot of money to anyone?"

Victoria shook her head.

"I don't know him that well," she said. "I worked with him. And not even that closely. He was hardly ever here."

"When did you last see him?"

"End of last week. Friday, I think. He normally only ever came in on Fridays or Saturday nights. That's when the best girls were working."

"So, Vince liked the ladies?" Sam asked.

"You know that expression, 'Don't shit where you eat.'?" Victoria asked. "Vince shit all over the place."

"Well, that conjures up quite the image," Sam muttered.

"He didn't harass anyone or anything," Victoria added. "It wasn't like that. He could be charming in his old TV star way. Lots of the girls fall for stuff like that. They even knew his reputation."

"But figured it'd be different for them," Sam finished her sentence.

Victoria nodded. "And I'm stuck playing clean-up."

"So, he was here this past Friday," Sam said, steering the conversation back. "How was he acting?"

"I hardly saw him," she said. "He walked in as I was heading out. But now that I think about it, he may have seemed a little nervous. Anxious or something."

"How so?"

She shrugged. "Just fidgety. Looking around a lot. Probably nothing."

"You think he was skimming from the club?" Sam asked.

Victoria laughed.

"He'd have to get in line for that," she said. "Between the dancers and the bartenders, it's a wonder the club is still in business."

"Financial trouble?"

Victoria didn't answer. She became lost in her own worries.

"Shit, what are we gonna do now? If Vince owed money, they're gonna take it out of this place. It could shut us down."

The large man in black, who had been standing outside the door, knocked then stuck his head in the office.

"Victoria, we need you out front," he said in a surprisingly soft-spoken voice.

Victoria sighed. "What now?"

She stood up, signaling the interview was over. Sam pulled out a business card and handed it to her.

"Listen, if you think of anything else that could be of interest, please call me."

Victoria looked at the card and then up at Sam.

"What the hell am I gonna do with that? You think these pants have pockets?"

Sam nodded and awkwardly placed the card on the desk, then tagged behind the woman who was storming out of the room.

THE FIRST THING Sam noticed when they got back out to the showroom was that no one was dancing. The second thing was that the three patrons were glaring at Josh, who was sitting on a bar stool while four semi-nude women fawned all over him. They were all laughing as Josh autographed napkins and other random slips of paper.

"What's going on here?" Victoria yelled.

The women snapped up to the sound of her voice. Three of them immediately scampered off. One woman waited nervously for Josh to finish signing his autograph.

"Get back on stage, Glitter," Victoria said.

"Do you know who this is?" Glitter asked.

Sam noted that her body was, in fact, covered in glitter. Josh handed her the autograph and she squealed, kissing him on the cheek before returning to the stage.

"You gonna pay for that private attention?" Victoria asked.

"I was just sitting here," Josh said. "I didn't ask them to come over."

"Twenty bucks a dancer," Victoria said.

"Come on!" Josh protested.

"Get him out of here," she said to Sam. "Before we lose the only three customers we have."

Josh started to protest but Sam corralled him toward the exit.

28

THE TWO HAD BARELY CLIMBED into Sam's truck before the teasing started.

"Must be nice," Sam said. "Having women crawling all over you all the time."

"Trust me. It's not all it's cracked up to be," Josh said.

"Oh, cry me a river," Sam teased. "What an awful burden that must be for you."

"You're not doing too bad yourself" Josh said. "How did a schmuck like you wind up with a gorgeous, smart coroner like Carla?"

Sam laughed.

"Don't let her hear you call her that. She's the medical examiner. They're touchy about that."

"Good to know," Josh said.

He pulled a notepad from his back pocket and scribbled a note.

"Thank God she has bad taste in men," Sam said with a wink

"So, you find out anything in the club?" Josh asked while writing.

"Not yet," Sam said. "While you were out there being manhandled by strippers, I was getting a cold shoulder."

"Hey, I was working," Josh said.

"Oh, yeah. I could see that."

"Once again, you were talking to the wrong person," Josh said. "All management is thinking about doing is covering their ass. I, on the other hand, was talking to the soldiers on the ground."

"Oh, really?" Sam asked. "What did your soldiers tell you?"

"Well, Linda was pulling a double shift and working days because things are starting to dry up at the ol' Double Diamond," Josh said. "The dancers get paid in tips plus part of the house. And a week ago, the house started taking a bigger percentage."

Sam nodded, trying not to act surprised.

"And Sandy, the glitter girl? She told me that a couple of months ago, Vince came in all blustered up and started throwing money around. Buying drinks. Paying for lap dances. And he started making upgrades to the place. New lights. New sound system. And then, just as suddenly, it all stopped."

"Spending big here. Investing in the movie. Sounds like Vince came into some money and then ran out of it just as fast," Sam said.

"Sure seems that way," Josh said. "And from the way he was spending, my guess is he wasn't expecting the money well to dry up so quickly."

"He became a bad investment," Sam said. "But by then, he was in over his head. He got desperate. First, he begs for more time. Then he starts making his own threats. Maybe blackmail. Making lots of noise. He starts to become a liability to whoever loaned him the money."

"And you think that was Garrett?" Josh asked.

"That's my guess, but I need something a bit more concrete," Sam said. "Which is hopefully what we're about to get."

Sam's truck was still parked in the back of the lot, giving them a good vantage point of anyone entering or leaving the club. Right now, they watched as Victoria stepped out the door and walked quickly to her car.

"I thought you said she didn't give you anything helpful," Josh said.

"I said not yet," Sam corrected. "You ever play pool?"

"Sure," Josh replied.

"Sometimes, when you don't have a good shot, you just hit the cue ball hard and see if any head for a pocket. Looks like our day manager is in a hurry, doesn't it? Let's see if she's headed toward a pocket."

SAM AND JOSH trailed far behind Victoria. Sam was very aware his classic truck would be easy to spot and pretty sure Victoria was driving scared. He almost missed it when she turned off into an industrial park and had to stay even further back as she navigated through the empty roads to a generic warehouse.

Sam pulled his truck to a stop a block away.

"I don't know what's inside there," he said. "You should wait in the truck."

"Like hell I am," Josh protested. "I can take care of myself just fine."

Sam knew there was no time to argue. He motioned for Josh to stay quiet and follow him.

29

SAM CREPT along the edge of the warehouse, Josh in tow, wary of any security cameras positioned outside of the building. He spotted Victoria's car parked next to a truck loading station. A large cargo truck was backed up to the open loading dock, but Sam didn't see anyone loading anything. For that matter, he didn't see anyone at all.

Motioning for Josh to crouch down and follow him along the edge of the loading area, Sam moved slowly, his eyes trained on the opening where he could see inside the warehouse. Confident they were alone, he moved up next to the truck and peered inside.

The warehouse was completely empty except for three rows of metal shelves near the loading area. The shelves were filled with large black duffel bags, giving Sam and Josh just enough cover to sneak inside.

They finally spotted Victoria. She was at the far end of the warehouse talking to a man who looked more like an insurance salesman than the hardened criminal Sam was expecting to see. As they watched, it was clear Victoria was upset. Sam's guess was that his visit had spooked her, and she was here to call off whatever shady business was going on at the club. When he had found she wasn't going to be very forthcoming, Sam had switched tactics and started asking questions. Nothing of importance. But enough to let her know he was curious and would probably keep looking. He knew she would want to cover her tracks but wouldn't risk a call. Phones leave a trail. Instead, she made a house call, inadvertently leading Sam and Josh right to them.

As Victoria continued to argue with the man, Sam reached up to one of the black bags and slowly pulled the zipper back. He wasn't that surprised to find large bundles of cash and, looking a little deeper, bricks of cocaine. He motioned at Josh to take a look but then froze as he felt the barrel of a handgun press into the back of his head.

He heard the click of the gun's hammer and then a whisper in his ear.

"You enjoying the show?" A man asked in a low, gravelly voice.

Sam turned to find Hector, Garrett's "security man" pointing a gun at him. He sighed and raised his hands in surrender. Josh did the same.

"Hey, boss," Hector yelled in the direction of Victoria and the mystery man.

The couple turned toward them, and Josh decided to take advantage of the shift in attention. He quickly spun around in an attempt to kick Hector's weapon from his hand. But his foot missed and Josh spun around uncontrollably, falling into the arms of his would-be victim.

"What the hell, man?" Hector grumbled as he pushed Josh to the floor.

Josh raised his hands in surrender, looking over to Sam who was staring at him incredulously.

"I don't understand," Josh said. "It worked when I played a UMC fighter once."

"Are you serious?" Sam shot back. "A movie?"

"I trained for months," Josh said. "I was good."

"Shut it," Hector barked. "Both of you."

"If you have to shoot someone first, pick him," Sam snarled.

"Seriously?" Josh replied.

Victoria and the mystery man walked over to Sam and Josh, both on their knees.

"You followed me?" Victoria yelled.

"I missed you," Sam said.

"Who are these two?" the mystery man asked.

"Private detectives, looking into Decker."

"Technically, I'm the private detective," Sam said. "He's just an actor."

The mystery man glanced nervously at Sam and Josh. He nodded at Hector, who took the cue and yanked Sam and Josh to their feet.

He forced them to follow the mystery man, who led them to a small office in the back of the warehouse. Hector pushed the two men into two wooden chairs facing a desk and shoved them around so they were sitting back to back.

"Here. Use this," the mystery man said as he threw a rope to Hector.

Hector bound each man's hands together and then their feet while the mystery man made a call. Then he wrapped another section of rope around Sam and Josh so they were tied together, back to back. Once he was confident, they were secured he took a step back behind them and waited for the mystery man to finish his phone call.

The man hung up and turned to stare at the two men.

"It appears our boss has plans for you," he said. "Such a shame. I was really looking forward to watching Hector put a bullet in your heads."

"Sorry to disappoint you," Sam said. "I don't think I got your name."

The mystery man smirked.

"I'm just a businessman," he said. "And you two are bad for business."

He grabbed Victoria's arm a little too tightly.

"The boss wants to meet with us," he said. "Back at the club."

Victoria tried to shake the man's grip from her arm, but he held on tight as he turned her around, leading her out of the office. Hector followed, grinning at the two men.

"I'll be back to finish this," he said. "I can't wait."

He shut the door and Sam and Josh sat helplessly as they heard the door being locked from the outside.

30

Sam and Josh jostled their chairs as they struggled to break free.

"Who was that?" Josh asked.

"I'm guessing that is the dealer that runs his merchandise through Garrett's club," Sam said. "Victoria probably came here to warn him."

Josh rocked their chairs back and forth.

"Would you stop it? You're going to knock us over."

"That's exactly what I'm trying to do," Josh said.

"Are you an idiot?" Sam asked. "We've got more leverage sitting up."

"I did this movie once," Josh explained. "When I pushed the chair over it broke and I was able to free myself."

"Jesus. Would you stop living in your movies? You see any cameras around? This is real life. People don't get knocked out from one punch. The ugly guy doesn't get the girl. And chairs don't break when you topple over."

Josh wasn't listening. He was intent on rocking the chairs

side to side. Sam tried to stop him by rocking in the opposite direction.

"That's the second time you've brought up a beautiful woman not liking an ugly guy," Josh grunted. "You get dumped a lot?"

"Once again. Real life."

Josh heard a small crack and looked at the legs of the chairs.

"We're doing this wrong," he said.

"Oh, so you know the secret to not getting dumped," Sam remarked. "I do recall a certain girl named Shelley."

"The chairs. You've got to push backward," Josh said. "That'll make me fall forward."

"That will also make me flip over you," Sam said. "Are you crazy? These are cement floors."

"You want to flip, or you want to face plant?" Josh asked.

"What?"

"You want to be the flipper-overer or the face-planter-under?"

Sam looked down at the chair's legs to see if he could figure out Josh's plan. Then it clicked. And he begrudgingly had to concede that it just might work.

"You flip over," Sam said. "I don't make a living from my face."

"Good point," Josh said. "Get ready."

The two began to rock in unison, Sam leaned forward while Josh pushed backwards and vice versa. They began to build up momentum.

"On three," Josh said. "One. Two."

He pushed backward with all his strength as Sam leaned forward. It was enough force that Josh began to flip backward over Sam. Sam's chair fell forward and Sam braced as his face hit the concrete floor hard. A sharp pain shot through his jaw.

Josh continued to roll over. As he did, the rope that was binding the two men began to loosen from the force of the movement. Josh used his legs to keep the chair flipping over.

"Aauugghh!" Sam groaned, as the force of their weight bared down on his face.

And then the momentum stopped. Instead of completing the rollover and breaking free, they just froze midway with Sam's face firmly planted on the concrete floor and Josh upside down.

"Shit," Josh said as his plan failed before his eyes.

They teetered for a second and then toppled to the side. The two lay there in defeated frustration.

"Well, hell," was all Josh could muster.

"Hang on," Sam said, as he began to wriggle. The rope that was wrapped around both of them had slid up to his shoulders and, with a little bit of shimmying back and forth, he was able to move it up even more so that it lay loosely around his neck.

"Start wiggling. Move the rope up," Sam said. "The one tied around both of us."

Sam could feel Josh wriggle. As he moved, the rope would tighten around Sam's neck, choking him.

"Hey! Human over here," he said. "Try not to choke me, alright?"

Sam could feel Josh moving frantically.

"It shouldn't be that difficult," Sam said. "Just wiggle side to side. Like you're using a Hula Hoop."

Josh started to wiggle more rhythmically, and Sam could feel the rope loosening. As Josh wriggled, Sam tried to look back and see what was going on, but he was stuck at an angle where he couldn't turn his head.

"Yes!" Josh exclaimed.

Sam could feel him pull free.

"Did you get out?" Sam asked. "How'd you get out?"

"Hang on," Josh said.

After a few more wiggles, Sam heard a crack and felt Josh completely pull away. As he stood, the rope pulled Sam's chair on its back, so Sam was helplessly looking up at the ceiling. He could barely see Josh snap the leg off the damaged chair. He still had rope bound around his wrists and ankles, along with broken pieces of the chair's arms and legs. But the pieces had been broken away from the chair so that Josh was free.

"How did you?" Sam was afraid to ask.

"The chair broke," Josh said with a smirk. "Just like in the movies."

He began to rummage the desktop and drawers.

"There's got to be a knife or something," he said.

Pulling open a desk drawer he laughed. He pulled out a large hunting knife with a ten-inch blade.

"These guys don't mess around," Josh said as he used the knife to cut the rope off of his wrists. Sam watched helplessly as the actor carefully sawed the blade through the rope.

"What are you doing?" Sam asked.

"I'm cutting off the rope."

"You're not cutting. You're sawing," Sam said. "Give it here."

Josh walked over to Sam, still laying on his back in the chair, looking up at the ceiling like an astronaut waiting for liftoff. He held up his bound hands to Josh.

"Put the knife under the rope with the blade facing out," Sam instructed.

Josh did as he was told.

"Now yank hard with a slight sliding motion," Sam said. "But not toward you. Away from you. And me."

Josh did as Sam told him and in one motion cut the rope free.

"Son of a bitch," he said in wonder.

"Give me the knife," Sam said, waving his newly freed hand at Josh.

Josh gave him the knife and Sam quickly cut away the rope on his other wrist and then his ankles. He handed the knife back to Josh and stood, rubbing his face.

"That floor is hard," Sam grumbled.

Josh quietly jiggled the door, but it was locked.

"What now?" He asked.

Sam took a few steps back and shrugged.

"Let's hope things keep working like they do in the movies," he said.

And then he ran at the door, throwing the full weight of his body into his shoulder as he slammed into the door. The door flew open, breaking free from the wooden door frame. The momentum sent Sam flying through the air and he landed on the floor with a thud. Josh walked through the open doorway and helped Sam to his feet.

"Just like the movies," he said.

31

RAMIREZ SANK BACK in they metal chair with a heavy sigh as another member of the film crew entered the room. To avoid the hassle of transporting crew members to the police station, Guzman had talked Ramirez into conducting interviews at the movie set. He had even set up a private space next to the costume department. Two folding chairs and a folding table that barely fit between rows of Bigfoot costumes, police uniforms, torn and bloodied clothing and other various costumes. A large metal fan roared in the corner, circulating the room's hot, musty air.

The newest interviewee was Brian, the production designer who had been working on the fake caves the night before. He nodded nervously at Ramirez, avoiding direct eye contact. Ramirez motioned for him to sit down.

"Name and job," Ramirez said as he leaned up to write on a yellow pad of paper laying on the table.

"Brian Parson. Production design."

"So you build those caves out there?" Ramirez asked.

Brian nodded.

"Yes, sir. Well, me and Matt. He's the head of the department."

Ramirez didn't care. The interviews had been going on for a few hours now and had been nothing but a waste of time so far.

"You know why you're here?" Ramirez asked.

"I, I think," Brian replied.

"You think?"

Brian started to sweat and shift in his seat. Ramirez could tell something wasn't right.

"What is it you think you're here for, Brian?"

Brian grew even more nervous, trying to figure out how to answer the question. Finally, blurted out his response.

"I swear. It was just that one time. And it was only because we were working so late."

Ramirez looked up from his note pad, confused.

"What the hell are you talking about?" he asked.

Now it was Brian's turn to be confused. He was sure he was being brought in because someone had found out he and Matt were smoking pot the night before.

"This is about last night, right? About me and Matt?"

Ramirez decided to play along.

"You tell me, Brian," he said. "What happened last night?"

"You mean, you don't..."

"I want to hear it in your words," Ramirez bluffed.

"We didn't even smoke that much, I swear," Brian said. "I don't know where it came from. Matt had it. And no one was around."

"What were you smoking, Brian?" Ramirez asked.

He now realized Brian's crime wasn't anything serious, but he was just bored enough to drag it out a bit.

"It was... just a little weed," Brian stammered. "But I swear. It was just a little and then we stopped. We didn't think anyone else was here or we never would have done it."

"Someone else was working late?" Ramirez asked. "Did they catch you? Did they tell you they were going to turn you in?"

"No. I didn't think she even knew we were there," Brian said. "I'm really sorry. Please. I need this job."

Ramirez raised his hand to stop him.

"I'll see what I can do," he said. "Tell me more about this other person you saw."

"It was that actress, Chloe Bernard," Brian said.

"She working late, too?"

"She was yelling at someone," Brian said.

That got Ramirez's attention.

"Yelling? Who was she yelling at?"

"I couldn't tell. But she was pissed."

"Could you hear her? What did she say?"

Brian shrugged. His adrenaline was still pumping, but he wanted to be cooperative so he could get on the detective's good side.

"Something like 'You owe me.' And 'You don't want me mad at you.'."

"Who was she threatening, Brian?"

Brian shook his head.

"We couldn't see."

"Was it a man? A woman? A group of people?"

"I don't know, sir," Brian said. "We were in the cave and she was on the other side of the warehouse. I only knew it was her because she walked past us when she left."

Ramirez tapped his pen on the notepad. Someone yelling at someone else wasn't exactly a break in the case, but it

could be something. At the very least, it was worth a
follow up.

He stood, signaling to Brian that the interview was over.

"I'm going to let your little indiscretion slide, Brian,"
Ramirez said. "But let's not let it happen again. Got it?"

Brian nodded enthusiastically.

"Thank you, sir. I promise, sir. Clean and sober all the way."

"One last thing. Do you know if Ms. Bernard is on set
today?"

Brian thought for a second.

"I don't think I saw her name on the call sheet," he said.
"She's probably at the hotel."

Ramirez nodded and waved Brian off. He decided to pay a
little visit to Chloe Bernard and find out who she had been
threatening. He doubted it had anything to do with the murder,
but it would give him a change of scenery and some air-condi-
tioning.

32

SAM PULLED into the parking lot of the nail salon that sat adjacent to Double Diamond's Gentlemen's Club.

"That's Garrett's car there," Sam said, pointing to a big black SUV in the strip club's parking lot.

"How can you tell?" Josh asked.

"Trust me, okay?" Sam replied. "At the very least, it's our boy Hector's SUV. I never forget a car that follows me.

"He said he was taking her back to the club to meet the boss," Josh said.

"That means Garrett's inside, which doesn't bode well for Victoria," Sam said. "They're probably in the back."

"Good luck getting back in there with all those big goons in every corner," Josh said.

Sam smiled. "That's where you come in."

JOSH OPENED the door dramatically and looked around the club. There were a few more patrons than before but it was still pretty dead.

"Ladies, I'm back!"

He swaggered up to the bar, nodding at one of the familiar giants that immediately stepped out of the shadows.

"Hey, Chewbacca. I don't want any trouble. Just came to apologize."

Josh turned toward the stage, acting as confident as ever but really buzzing with nerves and adrenaline. One of the dancers he had met earlier, Glitter, was on stage. She smiled wide as she recognized her newest customer.

"Hey, Glitter," Josh said. "Miss me?"

Josh pulled up a chair next to the stage and pulled out a twenty-dollar bill, kissing it before tucking it into Glitter's G-string. A few more of the goons emerged from the shadows, stepping toward the actor they had kicked out earlier the same day. One of them tapped Josh on the shoulder.

"Sir, I thought we were clear earlier. You need to leave."

Josh turned to the large man, acting shocked and innocent.

"Oh, man. I'm sorry. I thought it was my friend that was the problem. But I ditched him and came back. I hope it's okay."

The large man waved another man over.

"Maybe we ask your boss if she minds," Josh continued.

"She's busy," the large man replied.

As Josh continued to bargain with the growing number of goons that were surrounding him, Sam snuck in and slid along the edge of the dark room toward the backstage door. Luckily, the security guard that stood watch had moved toward Josh as well, leaving the door unattended so Sam could slip inside.

When Hector had caught them earlier, he was so sure his

captors wouldn't be able to break free from his rope that he didn't even bother taking Sam's pistol. Sam now held it in front of him as he retraced his steps from when Victoria had led him back to the office earlier. As he neared the dressing room, he could hear Garrett's voice.

He peered around the corner into the dressing room and saw Garrett standing over Victoria, who was being held down in a chair by Hector. There was blood on her lip from where Garrett must have hit her. Sam was about to barge into the room when he stopped himself.

I may be able to get some concrete evidence this time.

He quietly pulled his phone from his pocket and, as Garrett continued to yell at Victoria, Sam recorded the conversation.

"I don't care if the police didn't show up," he yelled. "I guarantee you they will. The fact is, you let yourself be followed and now the operation has been compromised. We're going to have to move locations and that's going to cost me time and money. Two things I hate to lose."

He motioned at Hector, who pulled a gun from his shoulder holster and aimed it at the woman's temple. Sam fought the urge to break up the party. He needed more information. Garrett wasn't going to shoot her yet. He was just threatening her.

And if things escalate, I can break in before it gets out of hand, he thought.

But before Garrett could say anything else to implicate himself, Sam's phone started buzzing. He looked down at it in horror. Carla was calling him. Sam scrambled to cancel the call and wound up dropping the phone. It hit the tile floor with a clatter and slid where Garrett and Hector could see it. Knowing he'd just blown his cover, Sam was left with no choice. He spun around with his gun held in front of him.

"Freeze!"

Hector already had his gun raised in Sam's direction.

"Oh, Jesus. It's you," Garrett said.

He was more exasperated than threatened.

"Put your gun down, Kojak. Or she dies."

He nodded at Hector, who put his gun back to Victoria's temple.

"Well, that's kind of an empty threat," Sam said. "You were about to kill her anyway."

"Maybe I don't have to," Garrett said. "Maybe you can do the smart thing and drop your weapon and then you can both walk away."

With his gun still locked on Hector, Sam glanced down at his phone. He saw the red light that indicated it was still recording.

"I don't understand why you have to kill her in the first place," Sam said.

"I don't let anybody get in my way," Garrett said. "Ever. She's not the first and won't be the last."

"What's to stop me from just shooting your goon?" he asked before turning to Hector. "No offense."

"You know as well as I do that he'll still have time to get off a shot before he falls," Garrett said. "And he's got his target squared up pretty nicely."

Hector pushed his pistol into Victoria's temple hard. She began to sob uncontrollably.

"You don't care that he's willing to sacrifice you like that?" Sam asked Hector.

Hector seemed to think about it for a second. He hadn't looked at it that way.

"There's one problem with that theory," Sam said.

Then, without warning, he fired. The first shot hit Hector in the shoulder of the arm holding the gun. His hand flew back involuntarily so when he shot his gun, the bullet went into the ceiling. Before he could recover, Sam fired a second time, this time hitting him in the chest. Hector toppled backwards and fell to the ground. Sam spun his gun around to aim it at Garrett, who had already raised his arms in surrender.

"I'm a good shot," Sam explained.

"You are making a big mistake," Garrett said with a smile. "You're out of your jurisdiction."

"Oh, I have no jurisdiction," Sam replied. "I'm not even a cop. But I do have a nice recording."

He reached down to pick up his phone, showing Garrett that the entire incident had been recorded.

Josh was cornered against the bar, nervously negotiating with a pack of club security guards. They all turned as Garrett walked through the back door, his hands linked behind his head. Sam walked behind him, his gun pointing into Garrett's back. Victoria hobbled in last.

"Call 911," she yelled at the security men. "Now!"

They all scrambled for their cell phones at once, but Victoria wasn't done.

"Did you not even hear the gunshots?" she yelled. "What do I even pay you for?"

As she continued her tirade, Sam walked Garrett up to Josh and tossed him a pair of handcuffs.

"Thought you'd like the honors," he said with a grin.

Josh looked at the cuffs in disbelief and wonder.

"You serious?" he asked.

"Go for it," Sam said.

Josh stood and closed his eyes, taking a deep breath.

"What the hell is he doing?" Garrett sneered.

"Getting into character," Sam replied.

Josh threw his shoulders back and turned toward Garrett. He seemed like a different person. Cocky. Sure of himself. He walked up to Garrett and spun him around, pulling his arms down and behind his back.

"James Garrett, you are under arrest for assault and battery, and a whole host of other charges, quite possibly including the murder of Vince Decker."

"Decker? Are you kidding me? Hey! You can't arrest me," Garrett yelled. "Neither one of you."

"You're going down the river, buster," Josh said.

He flinched at the line and turned to Sam.

"Too much?" Josh asked.

"Maybe just a tad," Sam replied.

Josh nodded appreciatively then snapped back into character, locking the cuffs on Garrett's wrists.

33

WHEN THE DALLAS police showed up, Sam filled them in on all they had witnessed. He admitted to shooting Hector, but Victoria backed up his claim of self-defense. Hector had also survived the shooting so, given the criminal's criminal background, along with Sam's non-criminal record as a police officer, the Dallas P.D. felt no need to arrest Sam.

Victoria almost immediately began positioning for a plea deal. Between her testimony, Sam's phone recording and the evidence they had found at the warehouse, much less anything else they would find at Double Diamond's, Garrett was going away for a long time. Not to mention Decker's murder. And Garrett didn't have the same pull in Dallas as he did in Quinton, so it was all more likely to stick.

Sam and Josh followed the police to the precinct and gave official statements. By the time they finally started heading home, it was getting dark.

~

JOSH HAD CONTINUED to play it tough through the police interviews and subsequent arrests. But they had barely driven out of the parking lot before he dropped the cool cop act.

"That had to be the single most cool thing I've ever done in my life," he said, finally releasing the excitement he'd been containing for hours. "I mean, did you see me?"

"I was there. Yeah," Sam replied.

"Other than that last bit, I did okay, right?"

"You were very believable," Sam said.

"I can't begin to tell you how grateful I am you gave me that moment," Josh replied. "I feel like, in that moment, I finally clicked with my character. You know?"

"I have no idea what you're talking about," Sam said with a grin.

Josh smiled and nodded.

"No. I'm not buying it," he said. "You get it. You wouldn't have given me that if you didn't."

Sam smiled.

"It is quite a charge," he said. "Bringing down a bad guy."

They drove in silence again, each taking in their own glory moment.

"You miss being a cop?" Josh finally asked.

Sam was surprised by the question and more surprised that he couldn't come up with an immediate answer.

"I think so," he finally said. "But I don't miss the bullshit."

For some reason, he wanted to change the subject, so he turned on the radio and twisted the dial through the static until he settled on a classic rock station. The two enjoyed the music for a while until Josh finally broke the silence.

"You think Garrett will confess to Decker's murder?" Josh asked.

"No chance in hell. But hopefully Hector may be willing to negotiate. Or maybe Victoria knows more than she told us. But now we know it was about more than just owing Garrett money. He was laundering drugs and money for him. My guess is that Garrett forced that operation on Decker in lieu of payment. Or as part of the deal. Either way, Decker was throwing more than idle threats at Garrett. He had some legit blackmail and could easily have made Garrett's life hell. If that's not a motive, I don't know what is. Still..."

"Still what?" Josh asked. "You're not sure?"

Sam shrugged.

"Garrett has the means. And the motive. But it just doesn't make sense," Sam said. "For one, Decker's body was found. If Garrett did it, he'd make sure the body stayed hidden."

"Maybe he just got sloppy," Josh said.

"Maybe," Sam replied. "But Garrett is never sloppy. And to get rid of the body on a movie set would be plain reckless. That's not his M.O. But... maybe the gator carried the body further than Garrett planned. Maybe someone stumbled upon them and they had to act quick. But..."

"But you don't think so," Josh interjected.

"Ah, what the hell do I know," Sam said.

A southern rock song came on the radio and he turned it up, drumming along with his hands on the steering wheel.

"Can I ask you another question?" Josh asked.

"Can you wait until this song is over?" Sam asked back.

"Are you worried about the Replacement Killer coming back?" Josh asked, ignoring Sam's request.

Sam stopped drumming his fingers.

"Guess you read about that," he finally said.

"Who didn't?" Josh asked. "That's wild stuff."

"Ken Mullen was my partner," Sam sighed. "I prefer to think of him that way. Not the name he gave himself."

Josh studied his driving companion. Sam didn't even crack a smile.

"Still, you've got to admit, he's turned out to be a lot more than just your ex-partner," Josh said.

Sam nodded. "I won't turn him into a legend, though. He's just a man. One I know well."

But Sam was lying. He didn't know who Ken Mullen was anymore. The man who was his partner in Houston years ago would never be a serial killer. He wouldn't have murdered those women. Women who had slipped through the cracks. Fallen off the grid. He had been their helper, not their stalker. Too many times, Sam had seen Ken go out of his way to take care of these women. Making sure they found a place to stay. Connecting them with lost family — on his own dime. That man was not the same person as this sadistic killer who would torture and kill his victims; who was so devious and arrogant that he would taunt the police by leaving an earring of the next victim on the ear of his previous victim. Sam had spent months trying to reconcile the two people and it still didn't make sense.

"So do you think he'll come back?" Josh asked again.

"I pray to God he doesn't."

34

OFFICER DANIELS OPENED the front door and casually walked through the home, Carla walking behind him. It was a routine she had gone through every day for the past several months.

Ever since Sam and Carla had received the threatening note from Ken Mullen, the police routinely drove past the house several times a day. And if Sam wasn't home, one of the uniforms would follow Carla home and do a sweep of the house. It had become such a routine that everyone, including Carla, went through the motions as if it were as normal as taking out the trash.

"I saw Sam the other day," Daniels said as he looked room to room. "When's he gonna make you an honest woman?"

"We're working on a date," Carla replied. "But you know Sam."

Officer Daniels chuckled as he continued his sweep. Carla went to the kitchen to pour a glass of wine. She had spent the day sifting through the human remains that had been pulled from the hungry alligator, as well as some water-logged remains that had been dredged from the pond. Still no head, but the pieces that had been recovered were beginning to tell a story.

It seemed Decker had taken a single shot at close range by a 9mm pistol in the chest. From what Carla could make of the arterial bleeding, it was that shot that killed him. The body had been cut up shortly thereafter, probably within an hour or two, and then the pieces were tossed into the gator pond. Due to the lack of blood on the banks of the pond, it was most likely Decker had been killed and chopped at a different location.

Unfortunately, no bullet was recovered so it would be impossible to do a ballistics match. And since 9mm pistols were the most common handgun in the country, it would be hard to narrow down their suspect list.

The saw used to cut up the body was a different story. From the splintered bone and ragged tears, she could tell the killer had used a hack saw. This told her two things. One, the killer was strong. Cutting up a human body is hard work. Cutting through bone, even along joints, was incredibly difficult. Two, the killer had time. Based on the number of recovered pieces, Decker's body had been cut into a dozen pieces. To do that with a hacksaw would take a couple of hours, at least. Since the time of death was between 1 and 2 a.m., the killer would have been busy cutting and disposing of the body until 4 a.m. at the earliest. This could be helpful as Ramirez and Sam followed up on the suspects' alibis.

"All clear, Carla," Daniels said. "You have a nice night."

"Thanks, Bobby," Carla said. "Say hello to Suzy and the kids."

As she sifted through the mail, she heard the front door shut and the patrol car drive away. Sam had called to fill her in on the day, so she knew he wouldn't be home for a couple of hours yet. That meant she would have some much needed alone time. For dinner, she would make herself a nice, light salad. Something that would never be enough of a meal for Sam. Then she would pour another glass of chilled wine and take a long, relaxing bath.

She put some music on the Bluetooth speaker — the kind of soft pop that drove Sam crazy — and smiled at the thought of Sam pretending to be in pain every time he heard one of the ballads.

As she started to pull the ingredients for her salad out of the refrigerator, she recalled the excitement in Sam's voice as he recalled his day. It was nice to hear him energized by something again. His obsession with Mullen had become worrisome and, as awful as the Decker murder case was, she was grateful he had been hired to work on it.

She pulled the cutting board and a chef's knife from a cabinet and set them on the granite countertop. She began chopping the carrots into bite-size pieces, the knife knocking rapidly on the cutting board, when something in her peripheral vision caught her eye. Something was leaning against the outside of the sliding glass door that led from the kitchen to the back deck. It was a white envelope.

A jolt of fear shot through her, and she clutched the knife tighter. She didn't remember seeing the envelope when she walked in, but Officer Daniels had checked the entire house— inside and out. There was no way he could have missed it.

That meant it had to have just been left there.

She slowly stepped toward the door, looking out on to the deck and the small, wooded area beyond it. It was already dark enough that it was hard to see anything.

Wait, she thought. *Wouldn't the motion-sensor security lights have tripped on if someone walked on the porch?*

Her breath caught in her throat as she answered her own questions. The only reason the lights wouldn't come on would be if someone had disabled them.

Her instincts were to run to the back of the house and call 911. But her scientist's curiosity drew her to the envelope. She clicked the levered lock on the sliding door, holding the knife out so she could attack anyone that jumped out at her. She slid the door open slowly, ready to slam it shut at the slightest movement. The envelope fell into the room and Carla pulled it into the house with her foot, immediately slamming the door and locking it. She stared at the envelope on the floor, her heart pounding.

Maybe it was nothing. It was a nondescript envelope with nothing printed or written on it. It could be from the power company. They were constantly sending notices about work they were doing along the back perimeter.

But why leave it at the back door?

Her rational forensics mind kicked in and she grabbed a pair of latex gloves from a box in the pantry. She also set down the knife and grabbed the pistol she kept in her purse.

The flap of the envelope wasn't sealed. And, as she picked it up, she was surprised how light it was. In fact, she began to wonder if there was anything in it. But then she felt a small object inside.

Her stomach flipped. Taking a deep breath, she opened the envelope and turned it over, letting the contents fall on to the counter.

Just as she had feared, it was two mismatched earrings. The deadly calling card of Ken Mullen, The Replacement Killer.

Carla backed away from the pearl earring and small, gold starfish earring. She felt dizzy and began to hyperventilate as she scrambled to find her phone in her purse, her eyes glued to the menacing pieces of jewelry staring at her.

She dialed Sam's number, quietly pleading for him to answer quickly.

35

RAMIREZ WAS TAKEN ABACK when Chloe Bernard entered the makeshift interview room. Her hair was unkempt and matted with dirt and weeds. Her makeup was smeared and her exposed arms, legs and mid-section were covered in bloody scratches. He knew it was for the movie. It had been made clear that he only had ten minutes with her while they relit one of the scenes, but it was more realistic than he had expected. And she still managed to be incredibly sexy. Of course, it didn't hurt that she was wearing nothing but a sports bra and a pair of very tight, very short shorts.

"Can I get a robe or a shirt or something?" she yelled back at the young woman who had walked her in.

"They don't want to mess up your makeup," the woman replied.

Chloe rolled her eyes as she sat down.

"Such is the glamorous life," she smirked, waving a hand over her body.

"Ms. Bernard, I'm sorry to bother you while you're shooting. This won't take long," Ramirez said.

"I already gave my statement," she said. "I don't know what else you could need."

Ramirez waited a minute before saying anything else. It was an interrogation trick he had learned a few years back. Before asking any questions, pause to notice the subject's demeanor. Do they act nervous? Calm? It didn't matter as much as it set a baseline on which to judge their reaction to any questions. Chloe sat cross-armed, drumming the fingers of her right hand on her left arm. She stared at Sam impatiently, waiting for him to speak.

So her baseline is 'annoyed', Ramirez thought.

"Detective, please tell me you didn't bring me in here to just stare at me," she finally said.

Ramirez chuckled.

"No, ma'am," he said.

"Here's a tip, detective... Ramirez, is it? Never call a woman 'ma'am'. Makes us feel old."

"Really?" Ramirez asked. "I was just being polite. No, sir. No, ma'am. Is that just a southern thing?"

"Maybe. But, trust me," Chloe said. "Use 'miss'. You can't go wrong by aiming young."

Ramirez nodded.

"Noted," he said. "Except, 'No, miss' sounds awkward."

"Then just say no."

Ramirez shrugged.

"So, Miss Bernard, can you tell me where you were last night?"

He purposefully threw out the question to see if it would throw her off. But Chloe only looked slightly confused.

"Can you be more specific? I was in bed by ten, if that's what you mean? Early call time this morning."

"Before ten," Ramirez said. "Around eight."

Chloe nodded.

"I had dinner with Chad McGinn, the director, to go over some dialogue. Then I stopped here to talk to Alan."

"Alan Guzman," Ramirez confirmed. "The producer."

"Slimeball is more like it."

"Can you tell me what you and Mr. Guzman were talking about?"

"I was giving him a piece of my mind," Chloe said. "I signed on early for this masterpiece. Guzman needed a name to attract investors and my agent owed him a favor. And it worked. None of this would be here if it weren't for me. And I think that deserves a modicum of respect, would you agree?"

"So you got into an argument," Ramirez said.

"I wanted to make some dialogue changes but Chad was stonewalling me. I came here hoping Guzman would have my back. Talk to Chad for me. Instead, the little weasel acted like his hands were tied. But I could tell. He was just trying to write me off. I'm just another actress to him. Another woman to not take seriously. You have no idea what it's like."

"No, ma'am. I mean, no. I don't."

"We have to work harder. Talk louder. Fight dirtier. And then we get labeled as a bitch."

"Did you threaten, Mr. Guzman?"

Chloe rolled her eyes at Ramirez.

"Are you even listening to me?" she asked. "You're damn right I did. I mean, we both knew it was an empty threat. The worst I could do is walk off the picture. But then he'd sue me for breach of contract."

She took a deep breath to gather herself.

"What's this even about?" she asked. "What's all this got to do with the murder?"

"Have other people threatened Guzman? That you know of?"

Chloe laughed.

"Probably everyone on this set," she replied. "It's the only language he seems to understand."

A uniformed officer stuck his head in the room.

"Detective Ramirez? Can you come out here? It's urgent."

36

THE BLUE AND red police lights illuminated the driveway as Sam's truck barreled in. Sam bolted out of the truck and raced inside, Josh running behind him. Sam was panicked and out of breath as he ran inside, yelling out Carla's name.

Carla was directing a team of forensic experts, who were scouring the house for any evidence. As soon as the police had arrived, she had fallen into her medical examiner role out of habit. Partly because she didn't want to appear weak to her male colleagues, but also because it was a safe place to hide rather than face the fact that Mullen had been that close. But when Carla heard Sam's voice, her stoic persona instantly melted away. As Sam walked into the room, tears began to well in her eyes and she fell into his arms, suddenly unable to breathe.

"Are you okay?" Sam asked.

Suddenly unable to speak, Carla could only nod her head.

"Tell me exactly what happened," he said quietly.

As Carla recounted her steps from the moment she had

pulled into the driveway, Sam's detective brain started spinning. He started scanning the kitchen and the hallway. He saw the earrings in a plastic evidence bag on the kitchen counter. Not letting go of Carla, he walked into the kitchen to examine the jewelry.

"No note? No nothing?" he asked.

She shook her head.

Ramirez walked up to Sam. He had been talking to the FBI agents in the living room.

"We had a unit over here within five minutes of her call," he said. "And I've got a team out scouring the woods right now, but there is no sign of anyone, anywhere."

"But he was here," Sam snapped. "He's not a ghost. He had to leave some sign."

"Sam, I'm so sorry."

It was Terry Goldsmith, the FBI agent that had been heading up the search for Mullen. He had met with Sam several times as they shared information. Goldsmith put a reassuring hand on Sam's shoulder.

"We're gonna find him."

"Why is the M.O. different again?" Sam asked, pointing at the earring. "This is the second time he's sent notes with earrings. Usually, they're attached to a victim."

Whenever one of Mullen's victims was found, she was always wearing mismatched earrings. Over time, a pattern was discovered. Mullen would abduct one woman and hold her captive for several days, usually torturing her. He would then abduct a second woman. Once he had his "replacement," he would take one of her earrings and put it in an ear of the first woman before killing her. It was how Mullen had earned the nickname The Replacement Killer.

"Maybe something happened to the victim?" Goldsmith guessed. "Maybe she got away? It's the same signature of mismatched earrings. The pearl earring matches the one he had sent to you with his first note. The starfish is new. Could be a previous victim. Or could be his next,"

"He's just playing with us," Sam said.

"I've ordered DNA tests on both," Carla said. "But that takes time. Even if we expedite it."

"Sam," Ramirez said. "I need to tell you something."

Ramirez pulled him aside and told him about the missing sex worker.

"You should have told me immediately!" Sam yelled.

"It only happened earlier today," Ramirez said. "Hicks and Awbrey were going to check it out. If they sensed anything weird at all, I was going to call you. Then this happened."

"You knew he was targeting Carla," Sam said. "What were you thinking?"

Sam's blood started to boil. He didn't like being a pawn in anyone's game.

"I need some air," he said as he stormed for the backdoor.

He stepped over the forensics analyst who was dusting for prints and walked down the steps that led from the deck to the backyard. He felt sick and put his hands on his knees, expecting to vomit. As he slowly regained his composure, he began to think.

Mullen wouldn't go to all this trouble just to tell me he had another victim, Sam thought. *There's something else.*

He stared into the woods at the back of his yard, watching the flashlights from the search team bounce up and down in the darkness. A spotlight blast over the yard, lighting it up like a football stadium. He turned to walk back up the stairs to the deck when something caught his eye. There was something on the support beams of the decks' handrail. Sam immediately recalled Mullen's advice from when he was a rookie detective and he knelt to examine what appeared to be handprints on the backside of the support beams.

It had to be Mullen. And they weren't there by accident. There was no dirt or smudges of any kind on the envelope or anywhere else. These prints were a message to Sam. But what did they mean? Sam studied them more carefully. The dried areas were a dark color, the wetter areas were an army green.

Where would Mullen's hands get stained dark green?

Sam knew the answer before he could even finish the question. The swampy river bottoms. The water was covered in a layer of green muck that served as both a feeding ground for bugs and fish, and a hiding place for alligators.

But there were acres and acres of swampy waters in the river bottoms.

Was there any place where Mullen could hide a victim? A shack? An abandoned fishing cabin?

He could ask the park rangers. They'd know. He started to race upstairs and tell the others of his discovery, but then stopped himself. If Mullen had wanted everyone to know, he would have left a more obvious clue. He knew Mullen well enough to know that he didn't do anything by accident. This was a clue meant for Sam and only Sam. If Sam showed up with a full team, Mullen would kill his victim before they could even see him. Sam's stomach dropped as he realized that the victim's best chance would be if he went alone. But where?

Then he thought of another person who knew the river bottoms well. It was just a matter of getting to him.

37

SAM WALKED BACK into the house and was relieved to see everyone was occupied. Even Carla was huddled in a conversation with a forensic technician. The only one standing around doing nothing was Josh, which is what Sam was hoping for. He walked quickly and discreetly to Josh and grabbed him by the arm, leading him toward the front door.

"What are you doing?" Josh asked.

"Don't make a scene," Sam whispered. "We're leaving."

"Shouldn't you tell Carla?"

"Stop asking questions and come with me," Sam said. "Keep your head down, avoid eye contact, and head to my truck."

Josh nodded and followed Sam's lead, sliding out the front door, past a couple of uniformed officers on the front porch, down the driveway and into Sam's truck. Sam started the engine and backed out of the driveway quietly then pulled on to the road. He waited until the house was out of sight then hit the accelerator and took off.

"What is going on?" Josh asked.

"What's the name of that location scout you introduced me to?" Sam asked.

"Ben?"

"Will he be at the set?"

"I don't know. He should be. You mind telling me what's going on?"

"I need you to trust me, okay?" Sam asked.

Josh saw the earnestness in Sam's eyes and nodded in agreement.

SAM PUSHED OPEN the door to the movie set and began searching for Ben . Unfortunately, he had barely taken a step when the writer Richard Fowler rushed towards them.

"Is it true?" he asked. "Did you catch the killer?"

""You know where Ben Tiernon is?" Sam asked, ignoring Fowler's question.

"Probably back by the cave set," Fowler said. "So did you?"

Sam turned to Josh.

"I'm getting Ben," he said. "You deal with him. Tell him nothing."

Sam rushed toward the set, leaving a hapless Josh with an offended Fowler.

"What did he mean 'Tell him nothing.'?"

"It's still an open investigation," Josh bluffed. "I guess I'm not allowed to talk about it."

"You're not even a cop," Fowler said. "For that matter, neither is he. So did you get the guy or what?"

"We made an arrest," Josh replied.

Fowler let out a very audible sigh.

"And you're sure it's him?" he asked. "We don't have to worry anymore?"

"Worry? What did you have to worry about?" Josh asked.

"I got to thinking. What if it was some kind of serial killer, targeting the film crew."

"There's only been one victim," Josh said.

"So far," Fowler argued. "But what if Decker was just the first? We could all be in danger."

"First off, we made an arrest, so you don't have to worry about that anymore," Josh said. "Secondly, if a serial killer is targeting a movie crew, you're safe. He'd come after the actors first. Maybe the director. But not the writer."

Fowler nodded, taking some solace in the insult.

"Sorry. You know me," Fowler said. "Imagination always spinning. So what's your detective pal all stressed out about?"

Josh looked up to see Sam leading Ben toward them. The location scout had rolls of maps tucked under his arm.

"Working on a different case," Josh said, as he stood to join Ben and Sam as they walked toward the door.

"It would be easier for me to do this here," Josh heard Ben protesting.

"We don't have time," Sam said. "You can look in my truck."

BEN SAT between Sam and Josh, unfolding sections of maps on the dashboard in front of him.

"I know there was something," Ben said.

"Where?" Sam asked.

"I'm looking!" Ben snapped back. "Here. I found it. It's an old observation post. In the southeast section of the preserve.

"Did you visit it? How big is it?" Sam asked.

"It's small. One room. Falling apart. Too small for our uses. I guess it was an observation station for a group of naturalists from Texas A&M about a decade ago. Way off the beaten path."

A perfect place for Mullen to hide, Sam thought.

"Tell me how to get there," Sam said.

38

SAM CUT his headlights and drove slowly along the red dirt road that cut through the river bottom forest preserve. Ben hadn't been exaggerating when he said it was off the beaten path. When they got close, Sam stopped the truck. He'd hike it from here. Fortunately, the sky was clear and the moon was bright.

"You two wait here," Sam said.

"Bullshit," Josh argued. "I'm coming with you."

"If Mullen sees anyone but me, he's going to kill this girl," Sam said. "I need the two of you to call Ramirez and Goldsmith and fill them in on what's happened and where we're at."

He turned to Ben.

"You'll probably need to navigate them here. Can you do that?"

Ben nodded and looked out into the darkness.

"What if he..."

"He's not gonna bother either of you," Sam assured them. "He wants me. The way I figure it, it will take the cops about fifteen minutes to get here. By that time, I'll have either neutralized the situation or screwed it up really bad."

"Be careful," Josh said.

"Why start now?" Sam replied with a wink.

Sam got out of the truck and quietly shut the door, heading off in the direction of the observation shack. He knew the general direction and had hoped Mullen would have left a light on for him. But with no such luck, he had to walk slowly and hope to God he didn't spook up a sleeping alligator or water moccasin.

Sam pulled out his Glock 9mm. He had thought about keeping it hidden to keep things from escalating. But Mullen would know he wouldn't come unarmed. In fact, Sam's guess was that he was expecting it. But why? Was he wanting a shootout? Why bring him all the way out here? None of it made any sense.

Sam followed the faint trail deeper into the swampy woods. He scanned the shadowy terrain as he walked, taking in any detail that could help him find his way back. His senses were fully engaged and on edge, half expecting Mullen to step out from behind a tree at any moment.

Even though it was dark, he was still swarmed by "no-see-ums," a cloud of mosquitos, gnats and midges. The hot, humid East Texas air had barely cooled with the setting of the sun and it stuck to Sam's skin. He wiped the sweat from his eyes and was beginning to think Mullen's plan was just to get him lost in the swamp. His left foot sunk in mud and Sam felt the sludge ooze into his shoe. He tilted his foot as he pulled up to keep from losing the shoe, but it was so weighted down with muck that he had to hobble over to a tree stump and remove it. He shook as much of the mud out of the shoe as he could, then peeled off his soaked sock. As he slid his foot back inside the cold, wet shoe, he noticed a structure through a cluster of weeping willows. It was just as Ben had described it. No more than forty feet by forty feet, which meant no place to hide.

Sam inched closer and then knelt behind a fallen pine tree to get a better look. The cabin sat at the edge of a large clearing that faced a larger pond. There was no way to approach it without being seen. In fact, he would be a sitting duck. He was clearly being led into a trap, but if Mullen had someone in there, he needed to help her. The problem was, he didn't know if anyone was in there. Or if they were still alive. And, truth be told, Sam would still prefer to make it out alive himself.

If Mullen was here, he was surely watching. Most likely from inside the cabin. Or maybe from an outside vantage point. Sam surveyed the area, but the woods were too thick. Mullen could be anywhere.

Sam figured his best move would be to do what he normally wouldn't. The predictable Sam would head straight to the cabin, gun held in front of him, calling Mullen's name. His old partner would probably be expecting that version of Sam. So he would try something different. He crouched down and began to slowly crawl through the woods with the plan to come at the cabin from the other side.

After what seemed like an eternity but was probably only a few minutes, Sam made it to the other side of the cabin. From this vantage point, he could see a single window that appeared to be covered in old, yellowed newspaper. It looked dark inside and there was no apparent sign of life.

Then he heard something that sounded like a muffled voice.

A bolt of both relief and panic shot through Sam. He

couldn't wait any longer. He had thought through the options and he knew that Mullen was unlikely to harm him right away. He liked to toy with his prey and if he just wanted to kill Sam, there had been plenty of opportunities to do that already.

With his gun at the ready, Sam crept toward the unknown in front of him.

39

ENOUGH MOONLIGHT SHONE down on the cabin that Sam could see the cabin door was cracked open. He could hear a woman's muffled cries but couldn't tell if she was trying to get his attention, trying to warn him, or trying to fend off Mullen.

Sam stood in front of the door and took a deep breath. It was now or never. With his gun aimed in front of him and his finger on the trigger, he kicked the door open. Jasmine's muffled screams filled the cabin as moonlight flooded the small, dark room. The woman's hands were bound over her head, just in the same way Sam had found Mullen's previous victims. She was blindfolded with a black rag, and her mouth was duct taped. Unable to see who had just opened the door, she writhed and shook in panic.

"It's okay," Sam said as he ran toward her. "You're safe."

Sam scanned the small room. Mullen wasn't there.

Jasmine's moans dissolved into sobs of relief as Sam pulled the blindfold down. He immediately noticed her black eye but tried not to show any emotion. He carefully peeled the duct tape from her lips as she gasped in air.

"Are you alright?" he asked.

She weakly nodded and he looked around for something to help free her bound hands. Spotting a range of knifes and ice picks on a small table, his stomach churned in horror, but he quickly grabbed a knife and cut the blue nylon rope that had bound Jasmine's hands to the chain. She fell into him and he slowly lowered her to the ground. Knowing she was free, she began to sob uncontrollably.

"It's okay," Sam said to her, feeling helpless.

Then he felt a presence. Someone was watching them. He looked up at the window covered in newspaper just in time to see a shadow move away from it.

"You son of a bitch," Sam fumed.

He turned back to Jasmine, who had seen the same thing. The weakness in her tired eyes filled with terror.

"Please don't leave me," she said.

"Help is coming," Sam replied.

He stood and ran out of the cabin, racing to where he had seen the shadow just in time to see Mullen disappear into the woods.

He yelled out at his old partner before firing a shot in his direction. Then Sam ran after him. The swamp was thick and Sam struggled to find Mullen. Then a single shot rang out and bark exploded from a tree next to Sam. He dropped to the ground and saw Mullen running through the trees. Sam clamored back to his feet and ran after him.

The terrain was inclining up and the ground was getting dryer. Sam knew the area enough to know that there was high ground to the east of the swamp. That must be where Mullen is heading. He ran in a crouch from tree to tree, trying to stay covered in case Mullen shot again. Seeing the shadow of a man step out from behind a tree, Sam fired a shot and then immediately ducked behind a tree as Mullen shot back. Before Sam could get another shot, Mullen had darted off again.

As Sam ran in the direction where he saw Mullen, he could hear rushing water. He knew there were lots of small rivers and rapids in these woods and figured they must be near one. That's probably how Mullen was planning to escape. The water was close, so Sam needed to catch up fast.

"Come on, Sam. Is this the way to greet an old friend?" Mullen yelled from the darkness.

"Go to hell, Ken!" Sam shouted back.

Mullen replied with several shots in Sam's direction. Sam lunged behind some brush to avoid being hit.

"Carla is looking really nice," Mullen yelled. "You sure are a lucky man."

"I'm going to kill you," Sam growled.

Mullen laughed and Sam could hear branches crunch as Mullen continued to run away.

Sam ran after him, climbing up a ridge which opened to a small clearing about twenty yards deep. Sam could see Mullen's silhouette running away then stopping, as if he had reached a dead end.

It must be a cliff that overlooks the river. Sam grinned, realizing Mullen had literally run out of options.

Mullen turned to Sam.

"I guess you've left me no choice, old friend," Mullen said.

He raised his pistol toward Sam but, before he could get off a single round, Sam fired twice. He watched as Mullen toppled back with each shot until he fell backwards over the edge of the cliff and out of sight.

Sam froze in shock. Unable to believe it was over. After a second, reality overtook him and he raced to the edge of the cliff and looked over. Even in the darkness, he could tell it was a straight drop of at least fifty feet. The water raced below, crashing around rocks that jutted out of the ground. Mullen was nowhere to be seen.

Between the long drop and the jagged rocks, there was no way he could have survived the fall, even without being shot. Sam tried to gauge how fast the water was moving. Trees and the night's darkness made it hard to see anything beyond about twenty feet of river. It was highly likely the water could have carried Mullen's body out of eyesight by the time Sam got to the ledge. But it wouldn't have gone far. Mullen was a big man and his body would get caught between rocks or shallow water.

Sam grabbed a broken branch and drove it into the ground to mark the spot where Mullen had fallen. He could hear approaching sirens and needed to get back to the cabin to fill Ramirez in on what all had happened.

40

THE NEXT AFTERNOON, Carla gathered her purse and yelled out to Sam that she was leaving for work. She had taken the morning to make sure Sam was okay but saw there wasn't much more she could do. He could tell she was antsy, so he suggested she go to the morgue so she could be there if Mullen's body came in. Even though they both knew that federal agents would summon her to the scene as soon as they found his body. She was just as useful at home as she was anywhere. Still, he could tell she was growing increasingly restless. That was the difference between the two of them. When things got stressful, Carla needed to stay busy. Sam fell into a sloth-like state of do-nothingness. To be fair, he had been up all night helping the police search for Mullen's body and then dealing with police reports. If it wasn't for the adrenaline still pumping through him, he'd be sound asleep.

The FBI had taken over the search for Mullen's body. Figuring the river had pulled the body further downstream, they had set up a couple of blockades along the river. But eventually, they put the search on hold until daylight. Knowing they had K-9s, drone cameras and manpower at their disposal, all Sam could do was wait.

Even though Sam had defied official police orders in going after Mullen, Ramirez had decided to fudge the police reports to help protect him. After all, Sam had figured out where Mullen's next victim was being held and probably saved her life. And if they had all showed up at once, Mullen would have killed Jasmine on the spot. In Ramirez's eye, they had saved a life and put an end to the Replacement Killer. It was not the time to quibble over protocol.

While the police and FBI celebrated their victory, Sam slipped away from the station and drove home. He retreated to his office without even saying a word to Carla and began staring at the wall dedicated to Mullen's twisted legacy. He hadn't budged since. Part of him felt relieved that it was all behind him. Another part mourned the loss of his old friend. But what ate at him was the fact that he would never get the answers he wanted. What had happened to Mullen to turn him into such a monster? How long had he been this way? And the big one: what could Sam have done to stop him?

Carla kissed him on the forehead.

"Didn't know if you heard me," she said gently. "But I'm going into the station to get the morgue ready."

With the FBI involved, she knew the morgue would be a hotbed of activity when they brought Mullen's body in. She wanted to clear space, prep an examination table and make sure all the other corpses were dealt with.

Sam nodded, never taking his eyes off the wall. She decided it was best not to say anything else. She squeezed his shoulder then left him alone. It was easily another hour when he was startled by a knock on the open office door.

"Hey, hey, Cap'n," Josh said. "I saw your truck, so I figured you were here and I let myself in. Hope that's okay."

When Sam didn't turn around, Josh walked quietly toward him. He was immediately drawn to the murder wall. Josh whistled.

"Holy cow, man," he said. "This is hardcore stuff."

Knowing Josh wasn't going to just leave and not wanting to explain his feelings, Sam shook them off and stood up.

"This? It came with the place."

Josh grinned but, wisecrack aside, Sam remained somber.

"You're lucky I didn't shoot you," Sam said. "Trespassers beware."

"I called Carla first," Josh replied. "She told me I could let myself in. She kind of insisted."

Sam shook his head.

"She keeps leading young men to a life of crime. You know there's no going back for you now, right? She'll have you robbing banks by the end of the week."

"You know I once played a bank robber?" Josh asked.

But he could instantly tell that Sam wasn't in the mood. He let his voice trail off to silence.

"Don't you have Bigfoot to catch?" Sam asked.

He stopped to think.

"There is more than one, right? What do you call that? Bigfoots? Bigfeet?"

"I got the afternoon off," Josh said, ignoring Sam's remark. "So I thought I'd come see how you're doing. Maybe if you're up for it, you can fill me in on what all happened."

Sam sighed.

"You want some iced tea?"

41

ANA WAS LYING on the couch in her trailer, trying to catch a small nap between scenes, when someone began banging incessantly on the trailer door.

"Hang on," she yelled to the impatient knocker.

She stopped at the mirror next to the door and straightened her hair.

Always look your best, she thought. *You never know who could be on the other side of the door.*

The banging started up once again and Ana flung the door open.

"What the hell?" she snapped.

Chloe burst into the room, waving a stack of script pages.

"Did you know about this?" she demanded.

"Know about what?"

"The new pages."

Chloe shook the pages in Ana's face. From the way she swayed, it was clear she had been drinking.

"What are you talking about?" Ana asked.

"Don't play dumb," Chloe said. "You've been after my part since you were signed on."

"What the hell, Chloe. I didn't even know there were new pages."

She grabbed the pages from Chloe and skimmed through them. Ana instantly recognized the crucial scene. But the dialogue and big dramatic moment that had previously been written for Chloe's character were now going to Ana's character.

"I don't understand," Ana said.

"Have you been sweet talking Chad, too?" Chloe asked. "Sleeping with him? That would explain why he cast you."

"Screw you!" Ana yelled. "I get my roles on merit. On talent. I didn't sleep my way to any part, as hard as that may be for you to even understand."

Chloe picked up a glass of water and hurled it at Ana. Ana ducked and the glass shattered against the wall behind her.

"You're crazy!" Ana yelled.

"I don't care if you're fucking the director, the producer or even the writer, you do NOT take my scenes from me!" Chloe yelled back.

"You think I have the power to change the script?" Ana asked. "I had to fight just to get this trailer."

"Is that before you started fucking your way up the call sheet?"

"Trust me," Ana countered. "If I was screwing my way to the top, you wouldn't even have a role."

Chloe let out a primal roar and lunged across the trailer at Ana, knocking the two of them back on the couch. They wrestled and rolled, throwing sloppy punches at each other. Ana kicked Chloe off of her and she toppled backwards on to the floor. Both women lay back, emotionally, and physically spent.

"I swear I don't know anything about it, Chloe," Ana said as she tried to catch her breath. "I would never do that to you. I don't want that kind of reputation."

Chloe was also gasping for air. As she caught her breath, she lost some of her anger. But instead of replacing it with a sense of calm, she was hit with a tidal wave of insecurity.

"So why would they take that scene away from me? Am I not good enough?"

"Are you insane?" Ana said. "You're Chloe Bernard. This entire movie isn't good enough for you."

Chloe forced a weak smile.

"Thanks. But you know as well as I do that no one in our business is too good for anything."

Ana propped up on her elbows.

"Come on. Who would think you weren't good enough for this piece of shit?" she asked. "Everyone involved with this movie knows we are lucky to have you. I heard you're the reason this piece of crap even got financed."

"Well, someone doesn't think I'm capable," Chloe said, pointing to the script pages now littered all over the floor.

"Maybe it's not personal. Maybe they just think the scene works better if my character does the heavy lifting," Ana suggested.

Chloe looked at her in disbelief.

"I'm the heavy lifter," she said. "Don't ever forget that."

Chloe pulled herself up and started collecting the screen pages.

"Someone's got an ulterior motive," she said, glaring at Ana. "I'm going to go talk to Chad and get to the bottom of this."

"You really think that's a good idea?" Ana asked.

Chloe looked at her co-star suspiciously.

"Why would you think it isn't?"

Ana wasn't sure how to answer.

"And to think," Chloe huffed. "For a second, I thought you were on my side."

She stormed out of the trailer, leaving Ana stunned and furious.

42

GUZMAN FELL BACK on the couch in his trailer/officer, exhausted. It was early afternoon but had already been a long day. He had spent the day fending off an increasingly curious press, who had caught wind of the rumor that Vince Decker had died on set. That, on top of the constant reshuffling of scenes to accommodate the demands of the production designers and the local police department, as well as all the normal day-to-day juggling, had begun to wear on Guzman. He opened a sound machine app on his phone and turned it up loud, then pulled an eye mask over his eyes and took a deep breath.

Before he could fully exhale, there was banging at the trailer door.

"Give me five minutes," he yelled.

"Alan, I need to talk to you now!"

It was the all-too-familiar voice of a very angry Chloe Bernard. Guzman thought about ignoring her, but he knew she wouldn't give up easily. And even if she gave up now, she would catch up to him eventually. He sat up with a groan, took off the eye mask and turned off his phone's sound machine.

"Coming, my dear," he yelled, as he walked to the door.

Before he could fully open it, Chloe barreled past him, waving the script pages in front of him.

"What is this?" she demanded.

Before Guzman could even grasp what was happening, Chad barged in after her.

"Jesus, Chloe. Really? I told you I'd take care of it," he gasped, out of breath from chasing after the actress.

"Take care of what?" Guzman asked. "Is someone going to tell me what's going on?"

"You can't just have me written out of a scene without telling me," Chloe said. "I deserve more respect than that."

"I told her it's a misunderstanding," Chad said to Guzman.

"Really?" asked another voice outside the open door

It was Richard Fowler, the screenwriter.

"If you're talking about the script, why was I not invited to this meeting?" he demanded.

"It's not a meeting," Guzman said.

"How did you even know we were in here?" Chad asked.

"Did you do this?" Chloe asked him. "Who told you to make these rewrites?"

"Who put you in charge, Chloe?" Ana asked as she squeezed into the increasingly crowded trailer.

As they all began to yell over each other, Guzman backed against the wall, wishing he could escape without anyone noticing.

43

JOSH SAT across the kitchen table from Sam, listening intently as Sam retold the story of finding the woman in the cabin, then chasing Mullen into the woods until he finally shot him off the cliff. It took every ounce of energy in Josh's actor body to not take notes. But he asked all the actor questions.

"How did you feel? Were you out of breath? Or were you calm?"

"Was your pursuit driven by rage or a sense of justice?"

"When you fired at Mullen as he was cornered on the cliff, were you shooting to stop him or shooting to kill?"

Sam couldn't answer any of them. He could barely remember the details of what happened. What he did know was that, if he had to do it all over, he would have aimed at Mullen's legs instead of his chest. Aiming at his shins would have knocked him forward and not backward. But Sam followed his training. In a dire situation, you don't take a chance on precision shooting. You aim for the largest body part - the chest. Still, Sam had replayed the moment over and over, finding different things he could have done so that Mullen would have lived.

Unlike many other law enforcement officers, Sam didn't believe in capital punishment. But not for any altruistic reasons. He just thought it let the scumbags off too easy. A long life spent in a shit-hole prison was far more punishment than the sweet escape of death. And he was pissed that Mullen got off so easy. He wanted him to answer for his crimes. He wanted him to have to explain why he did it. He wanted him to have to live with the regret over what he had done for the rest of his life. And he would have made sure Mullen regretted it. He would have visited him regularly. And each visit he would have brought the picture of a different one of Mullen's victims. He would have told Mullen their story. The family that was left behind. The damage he did and suffering he caused to people that never deserved it. He had to believe it would get to Mullen. He had to believe he had a conscience buried in him somewhere.

As Sam told his tale to Josh, they were interrupted by Josh's phone. Seeing the number on his Caller ID, he decided to answer it.

"Yeah?"

The voice on the other end seemed excited and agitated. It only got a smirk out of Josh.

"No shit? Oh man, I'd love to be a fly on that wall."

He listened some more and nodded.

"Well, c'est la vie, man. What are you gonna do?"

He chuckled as he hung up the phone.

"I need to get back to set," he said. "I guess all hell is breaking loose."

"What's going on?" Sam asked.

"Some script change has got Chloe up in arms and it's getting elevated," Josh said, making air quotations to let Sam know the word choice wasn't his own.

"And you're going to fix everything?" Sam asked.

"I'm good at calming things down," Josh said with a sly smile.

Sam laughed and nodded.

"Seems pretty much of a non-issue," Sam said.

"Oh, no," Josh replied. "Cutting someone's lines is like an act of war. And blood is very likely to spill."

He got up to leave and Sam also stood.

"Know what? I'm gonna go with you," Sam said. "Something is still bugging me about this whole Vince Decker murder. I feel like we're missing something."

"Alright. But I gotta warn you. It sounds like the shit is hitting the fan hard."

Sam smiled.

"After all that's happened over the past 24 hours, I think I can handle a little fan shit."

44

FILMING HAD STOPPED for the day so the movie set was fairly quiet. A cleaning crew took advantage of the downtime to clean up the large warehouse. The whining drone of vacuum cleaners made it hard for Sam to hear Josh shouting directions, so he opted to just follow the actor.

As they walked, Josh's phone pinged again. He had been receiving non-stop texts since they had left. Some from Chloe asking where he was. Some from Ana asking if he can help calm Chloe down. Some from Chad asking him to stop by Guzman's office (but never saying why). And a few from other crew members warning him to stay away.

"Who's that?" Sam asked.

"This time it's Ana. She said Chloe stormed out of the fight. She's going with her to try to calm her down."

"That should lower the temperature a bit," Sam said.

"Or stop everyone else from holding back," Josh replied.

As they neared the side door where all the trailers were located, they could hear the yelling. Guzman's trailer door was open and Chad, Fowler, and Guzman were still locked in a heated exchange about the script revisions.

"I don't care if you're the producer," Chad said. "I'm the director. I'm the captain of this ship and I make the calls."

"I write the checks, Captain," Guzman said. "Check your contract. All major changes must go through me. To avoid this very type of disaster."

"This wasn't major," Fowler yelled.

"You took the scene from our marquee actor," Guzman said. "That is major."

Chad noticed Sam and Josh as they stepped into the trailer. He beamed proudly and put his arm around Josh, pulling him into the argument.

"There you are," Chad said. "I need to get your opinion on something."

"Oh. He gets a vote now? This is bullshit," Fowler said, taking his glasses off to pinch the bridge of his nose. "My head is going to literally explode."

"Jesus. That's a bit overdramatic," Chad said. "Maybe you should be an actor instead of a writer."

"Maybe you should be a human instead of a dick," Fowler shot back.

Josh stepped between the two men as they yelled threats at each other.

"Enough!" Guzman yelled. "We're switching the scene back and that's the end of it."

Chad and Fowler glared at each other, and Fowler finally looked away.

"I've got a plane to catch," Fowler grumbled before turning to leave.

"You can't just leave!" Guzman yelled.

"I'll fix the scene on the plane and email it to you. I have a meeting. I need to book my next gig before this heap of trash hits the screens."

Fowler bumped shoulders with Sam as he stormed out of the trailer. But Sam barely noticed. He had been too busy staring at Fowler's glasses.

45

As SAM PULLED Josh aside and whispered instructions to him, Guzman seemed to notice him for the first time.

"If you're here to get paid, you'll have to send me a bill," Guzman said.

"No," Sam replied. "I mean, yes. But no. I will, though."

Guzman looked at Sam as if he were crazy, then turned back to Chad.

"When is that scene scheduled to shoot?"

"Tomorrow morning," Chad replied. "I'll shoot around it. But if the crew stage a mutiny I'm tossing you at them."

"What about you, Josh?" Guzman asked.

But Josh and Sam had already left.

SAM LOOKED around the labyrinth of trailers for any sign of Fowler, but there was no sign of life. Then he heard the echo of steps in the movie set and he ran in, almost knocking Fowler down. The writer had a black travel back in one hand and a laptop case in the other.

"Oh, there you are!" Sam said. "You got your stuff fast."

"I don't want to miss my flight," Fowler said.

"Is Ana going with you?" Sam asked.

Fowler stopped and looked at Sam.

"Sorry?"

"I just figured," Sam continued. "Since the two of you are an item."

"I don't know what you're talking about."

"When I met you the first time. At the movie set. You weren't wearing those glasses," Sam said. "But at that point, they were still in Ana's room, weren't they?"

"I really need to get going," Fowler said.

"I bet you panicked when you realized you had left them there," Sam continued.

"Look, buddy. You're way out of line. You're not even making any sense."

The side door opened, and Josh walked in with Ana, just as Sam had instructed.

"Oh, look who's here," Sam said, never taking his eyes off Fowler. "Maybe she'll understand my question. Ana, were you and Fowler an item?"

Ana looked at Fowler nervously.

"It was just a fling."

"JUST a fling?" Fowler shot back. "That's all I was to you?"

"Richard, I didn't mean it like that."

"Was it a... what did you call your thing with Decker?" Sam asked. "A production fling?"

Ana looked at Fowler. "I'm sorry, Richard."

"After all I did," Fowler replied. "I even changed the script to give you more screen time."

"You did that?" Ana asked.

"You must really care about her, huh?" Sam asked. "I bet it really pissed you off when you found out she was also having a fling with Decker."

Fowler struggled for what to say next. Coming up with nothing, he dropped his bag and laptop case and took off. He ran toward the set, with Sam and Josh in hot pursuit. In a futile effort to escape them, Fowler ran through the cavern set and into a set of stored cavern sets behind it. One of them had a tunnel built into it and Fowler quickly scurried up and inside.

By the time Sam and Josh had raced behind the cavern set, Fowler was nowhere to be seen.

"You couldn't have gotten far," Sam yelled. "You know, we're going to find you."

Sam and Josh looked through the different set designs and Josh pointed up to the tunnel. They quietly walked along the outside of the set, following where the tunnel was leading. It emptied out on to a different, smaller cavern set. Sam motioned for Josh to go back to the entrance of the tunnel. Sam would wait at his end as Josh flushed Fowler out. Sam hid behind a large styrofoam boulder and it wasn't long before he could hear the panicked shuffling sounds of Fowler climbing out of the tunnel. Sam could have stepped out and grabbed the writer, but he knew he had a once-in-a-lifetime opportunity staring at him. As Fowler started his escape, Sam grabbed the giant boulder and threw it at the writer, grunting loudly as if the boulder was real and he was possessed with super-human strength. Fowler toppled to the ground and Sam ran over to him.

"That was awesome," Sam said, as he clicked handcuffs on Fowler's wrists.

Josh pulled himself out of the tunnel and ran over.

"Please tell me you saw that," Sam said.

Josh looked at Fowler on the ground and the giant boulder, still rolling back and forth.

"Please tell me you didn't throw that at him," Josh replied.

Sam pulled Fowler to his feet and started walking him toward the exit.

"Now where were we? Oh yeah. You were pissed off about your girl sleeping with another guy."

"I am not his girl," Ana yelled as she caught up with them. "I didn't cheat on anyone. We weren't exclusive. Why are you arresting him?"

"I bet you were walking down the hall just in time to see Decker leaving her room," Sam said, ignoring Ana. "That got your blood boiling, didn't it? So, you followed him. I'm guessing to the parking lot behind the hotel. Things got heated. Words were said. Blows were exchanged. And it got out of hand. Am I warm?"

Fowler fumbled for words, but nothing came out.

"What'd you use? A tire iron? A rock?" Sam continued. "I'm guessing you hit him over the head, which we never found, by the way. Then you stabbed him. Just to be sure. But you couldn't just leave the body out there. So, you threw him in your trunk, grabbed a hacksaw from one of the equipment vans and drove out to the swamp where you were filming. The one filled with alligators. Feel free to stop me at any time to tell me how brilliant I am."

"You're full of shit," Fowler said. "And even if it were true, you've got no proof."

Sam led Fowler out to the parking lot. Josh and Ana followed.

"Which car is yours?" Sam asked.

Fowler refused to answer so Sam reached into Fowler's pocket and pulled out his keys. He pressed the unlock button and the orange caution lights of a black Toyota Prius blinked.

"My guess is you used the trunk of your car as your chopping block," Sam continued, walking toward the car. "Man, that must have been bloody. Hard to clean all of that up. Mind if I take a look?"

Sam passed Fowler over to Josh as he walked to the back of the Prius. Josh, Fowler and Ana crowded behind him as he opened the trunk. Unfortunately, the inside was packed with luggage.

"Really?" Sam said. "You're really going to make me work for this, aren't you?"

Sam started removing luggage. But, with every suitcase, he grew increasingly surprised. The trunk was clean. No blood. No sign of any foul play.

"Go ahead and get your forensics people to check it for DNA," Fowler said. "The trunk is clean. You screwed up, Lawson. I'm not your guy."

Sam looked at Fowler, not sure how to respond. He was sure he had been right. What had he missed?

"Wait a minute," Josh said. "This is a rental, right?"

They all turned to the actor.

"You had a blue car two days ago," Josh said.

Sam smiled at Josh then turned to Fowler.

"Ricky, did you get a new rental car? I bet if we check the blue one, we'll find a very bloody trunk."

"I didn't mean for any of it to happen!" Fowler blurted out.

Ana gasped and took a step back. Fowler's shoulders sunk as he realized he was caught.

"You're right," he said. "I saw him leave Ana's room and I followed him. I was pissed. And, yeah, things got heated. He was an asshole. Started insulting me. He pushed my buttons and I just got so angry. It's kind of a fog after that."

"I get the heat of the moment fog," Sam said. "But you chopped his body up and fed it to alligators."

Fowler shrugged. "I panicked."

46

IT WAS LATER that evening and Carla was opening the door to the house when her phone started ringing. She rushed inside, putting her bag of groceries on the counter and fumbling for her phone at the same time. She saw the name on the Caller ID and sighed with a smile.

"You always know the perfect time to call," she said into the phone.

"Isn't any time the perfect time?" Sam replied, trying to sound suave. "Where are you? I came down to your office and you're not here."

"There's been no news yet," Carla replied. "I figured I'd come home and we'd have dinner. What are you doing at the morgue?"

"I've been at the station most of the afternoon," Sam explained. "Yours truly solved the Decker murder."

He told Carla how he had looked over at Fowler when everyone was arguing in the producer's trailer and noticed the writer's glasses resembled the pair that were in Ana's hotel room when he had first questioned her. He always had a feeling Ana was lying when she had said those glasses were hers, but so many other things happened so quickly, he had honestly just forgotten about it. Until he saw Fowler's glasses and realized they looked the same. Once he had made that connection, everything else fell into place.

Knowing she was about to get the full story in glorious, technicolor detail, Carla switched to speakerphone and unloaded the bag of groceries while she listened. Sam spared nothing, adding flourishes of color, and possible exaggerations, throughout the tale. By the time he was finished, the cheese tortellini was already boiling in a pot of chicken broth.

"So why are you still at the station?" she asked. "You don't do the processing anymore."

"I was mainly waiting to give my statement," he said. "Even with everything else that's gone on, Chief still has it out for me. I'm pretty sure he went out of his way to delay my interview as long as possible. Pretty much the entire cast of the movie gave their statement before I did."

"Ugh. I'm sorry."

"It's okay. It's Boston Kreme donut day here at the station. Plus, it gave me a chance to wrap things up with the movie people. I even got paid. In cash."

"Seriously?" Carla said with a laugh.

"Guzman referred to me as a petty cash expense," Sam said. "I'm pretty sure he meant it as an insult, but I've been called much worse and didn't get paid for it."

"I'm assuming Josh is with you?" Carla asked. "He called me earlier looking for you."

"Yeah. That's when you encouraged him to break into the house," Sam replied. "Josh is good. He's walking around the station taking notes. He's also asked if I can come on set as his technical advisor."

"Look at you, getting another job. I'm proud of you, hon. You're having quite the week."

"Cracked two cases and turned into a superhero who threw a giant boulder to catch the criminal."

"Dear Lord, I'm never going to hear the end of that, am I?"

"Too bad no cameras were rolling," Sam said. "When you're on those sets, they look so real. It's so easy to get caught up in it. You forget it's all smoke and mirrors."

As the words came out of his mouth, a terrifying thought flashed into his mind.

"Holy shit," he mumbled.

"Sam? What happened?"

"Hon, I've gotta go."

He hung up and ran to his truck.

47

SAM GOT to the river bottom preserve in record time. It was still swarming with police and FBI search teams. Sam ran through the woods to the clearing where Mullen was shot and spotted Agent Goldsmith.

"Do you have any climbers?" he asked as he tried to catch his breath.

"What are you talking about?" Goldsmith asked.

"Climbers. Someone to climb down the cliff."

"Everyone's downstream. We haven't found anything yet."

Sam walked to the cliff's edge and looked down, frustrated that he couldn't see what he was looking for. He looked up and spotted something flying through the air.

"A drone," he muttered to himself.

He ran back to Goldsmith.

"I need you to get one of those drones over here."

"What's going on, Sam?" Goldsmith asked.

"Just get the damn drone!" Sam snapped.

Goldsmith nodded and pulled a walkie talkie from his suit

jacket pocket. He spoke to someone, never taking his eyes off of Sam.

"An agent is coming over," Goldsmith said. "Do you mind telling me what's going on?"

Before Sam could explain his theory to Goldsmith, an agent ran toward them. He was holding a laptop-style device in front of him.

"Does that operate the drone?" Sam asked.

The drone agent looked at Goldsmith, who shrugged his shoulders and nodded his head.

"I need you to fly it down," Sam said, pointing to the place where Mullen had fallen over. "Along the cliff where he fell."

He ran over to the cliff's edge.

"Down here somewhere."

The drone agent nodded and used a toggle to control the drone that Sam had seen earlier. It flew toward them and then hovered as the agent lowered it out of sight.

Sam ran over to the agent.

"Can you see what it sees?" he asked.

The agent nodded again and pointed at a screen on the drone command device he was holding. Both Sam and Goldsmith stood behind the agent to watch.

"Damnit," Sam said. "You see that? What does that look like to you?"

The agent zoomed in closer.

"It looks like a large inlet in the cliff wall," the agent said.

"Like a mini cave, right?" Sam asked. "Enough for a person to hide in, right?"

"How did we miss that?" Goldsmith muttered.

"You can't see it from up here. The top of the cliff extends past it," Sam said.

"Wait. You think Mullen hid in there?" Goldsmith asked.

"Look. There's even a little bit of a ledge in front of it," Sam said.

"But you said he fell backwards," Goldsmith said. "Even if he tried, he couldn't have hit that ledge, much less climb inside of it before you got over."

"He could if he knew it was there," Sam said. "And he was secured."

He had the drone agent zoom in closer to the ledge and search until he found a shiny metal object embedded in the stone.

"That looks like a climber's piton," the drone agent said.

"A what?" Goldsmith asked.

"A piton. A spike that climbers drive into rocks," The agent explained. "It's got a hole they can run a rope through to secure them if they fall while they're climbing."

Goldsmith turned to Sam.

"You said that when Mullen ran toward the cliff, you were hiding for cover. For how long?"

"I don't know," Sam said. "Fifteen, twenty seconds?"

" If Mullen already had a rope tied to that piton and the rest of it sitting up here..."

"That would have given him enough time to tie the other end of the rope around his waist before I saw him," Sam interrupted. "When he fell backwards, the rope would have caught him and swung him right into the inlet."

"Then when you came back to get us," Goldsmith said. "he could have made his way along the cliff in the opposite direction. But you shot him. Twice."

"Maybe he was wearing a bulletproof vest," Sam replied.

"I don't know. I'm hearing a whole boatload of maybes," Goldsmith said.

"Take a look at this," the drone agent said. "Looks like some fragments of blue twine stuck on the piton. And if we move down..."

He directed the drone to pull back and move along the edge of the cliff.

"That looks like footprints, sir," he said.

"It was all smoke and mirrors," Sam said. "He staged the whole thing."

"While we were all searching downstream, he was escaping in the opposite direction," Goldsmith added.

Sam looked at the FBI agent, letting the horrific truth set in.

"He's still out there."

"But why? Why go to all of that trouble? We didn't know where he was. Then he shows up again just to lure you out here so he could get away again?" Goldsmith said.

"No. He lured me out here so I could watch him die. Because if we think he's dead, we'll stop looking for him," Sam replied.

"You want me to shift the focus of the search?" the drone agent asked.

Goldsmith held out his hand.

"Not yet. Do a search with the drones but let's keep this between us right now."

He turned to Sam.

"Right now, he doesn't know that we know he's alive," Goldsmith said. "That gives us the edge."

"The edge?" Sam asked. "So, we can just sneak up on him now? Except, oh wait, we have no idea where he's at. We're no better off than we've ever been."

"No. We are. We're going to report him as assumed dead. The alligators probably got him," Goldsmith said. "Only a select few will know the truth. If he thinks we believe he's dead, there's a chance he'll stop being careful. And when he slips up, we'll be ready."

"And until then, he's just running free out there?" Sam asked.

A wave of panic swept over Sam.

"Oh, God," he said, grabbing his phone. "I need to tell Carla."

48

CARLA PUT the empty bowl of tortellini soup in the sink. She'd clean up the mess later. Right now, she just wanted to get out of her work clothes. She kicked her shoes off and curled her bare toes in the carpet. Even though she had long ago traded in high heels for sensible sneakers, she still always felt instant relief when she took her shoes off. Because she was in a white lab coat all day, she typically just wore a T-shirt underneath, especially in the summer. She peeled off today's T-shirt and tossed it on the bed, enjoying the cool bath of air-conditioned air on her skin. She stepped out of her pale blue scrub pants, leaving them in a pile on the floor.

She wondered what was going on with Sam. She hadn't heard from him since he practically hung up on her. Probably just forgot something in the station and had run back in to get it. He'd probably be home any minute, ready to regale her once again with how he solved Decker's murder. And threw a giant boulder.

She caught her reflection in the full-length mirror attached to the bathroom door and turned to get a better look at herself. Carla had always been long and lean, although she could tell she had put on a few pounds. She considered it a by-product of living with Sam. She used to work out more. And eat healthier. But a little belly bump was a small price to pay for nightly snuggles with her man. She patted her stomach and smiled. It was only then that she realized the bathroom door was shut. They never shut the door. It was a signal that the room was occupied.

"Sam?"

She called out his name but knew he wouldn't answer. There's no way he could have snuck into the house without her knowing. And why would he? She thought again about how their phone conversation ended.

Maybe something was wrong.

She knocked on the door.

"Hello?"

The door hadn't been secured shut and it pushed open slightly when she knocked.

"Who's here?" she asked again.

Her purse, and her gun, were in the kitchen, so Carla stepped backwards slowly, never taking her eyes off of the bathroom. She reached back with her hands and felt for the baseball bat Sam had insisted on leaning against the wall next to the bed. When she felt it, she grabbed it tight and swung it around, holding it with both hands. She stood sideways, like a baseball player at home plate, as she inched forward toward the bathroom again. She stood in the doorway, looking inside. The room was empty.

But the shower curtain was drawn shut.

Carla crept toward the curtain, bat at the ready. Then, in

one swift movement, she yanked the shower curtain open with her left hand as she let out a ferocious yell—something she had learned in a self-defense class to throw off a would-be attacker. Without even waiting to see if someone was there, she swung hard and fast. But the bat hit nothing but air.

She looked at the empty space, her heart pounding through her bare chest. And, assured that no one was there, she began to laugh at herself.

"Well, better safe than sorry," she said out loud, grateful that no one had seen her.

Vowing to yell at Sam for shutting the door, Carla set the bat back next to the bed and returned to the vanity to remove her jewelry. She unclasped the gold crucifix necklace and laid it on the vanity counter then removed her emerald earrings and sat them next to it. She was meticulous about her jewelry and had a place for everything. Sam made fun of her accessory organization but it made it easier for her to find what she wanted in the morning. She opened the jewelry box lid and placed the necklace in one of the many velvet-lined trays that fit inside. She then slid open a drawer underneath the main section. It was divided into several small sections, each holding a different pair of earrings. She carefully placed the emerald earrings inside one of the empty sections but then noticed something odd.

One section contained a single blue gemstone earring.

Where was the other one?

She hadn't worn them in a long time but was surprised she hadn't noticed before. She slid open the two other trays and looked, then lifted the entire jewelry box up to see if the rogue earring was underneath. As she continued to check the counter, she could hear her phone ringing in the other room.

Probably Sam calling back, she thought. *Wondering what's for dinner.*

She ignored the phone and got on her hands and knees to look on the floor around the vanity. She prayed she hadn't accidentally vacuumed it up, but then reassured herself that the vacuum cleaner would have made a racket if that had happened. She stood, staring perplexed at the jewelry counter.

Then she felt a strange sense that someone was behind her.

She looked in the small vanity mirror on the lid of the jewelry box and saw Mullen standing behind her. Before she could even react, he grabbed her and pulled her back tightly against his large body. She watched in helpless horror as he lifted the other hand. It held a large syringe, the kind she knew he used to subdue his victims. She struggled but he was too strong, and she felt the prick of the needle piercing her skin.

The phone ringing in the other room grew more distant and muffled. And then everything went black.

THANK YOU

Thank you for reading DEATH ON LOCATION.

If you enjoyed it, be sure to leave a review wherever you bought
your copy. A review can go a long way in helping other readers
find this book.

GET A FREE COPY OF *BOUND BY MURDER*
This fun and riveting mystery novella e-book goes back to the
first murder case when Sam Lawson and Ken Mullen were
partners.
It's available for free at **davidkwilsonauthor.com**

ENJOY THESE OTHER SAM LAWSON MYSTERIES

COMBUSTIBLE - Sam Lawson Mystery 1

BENEATH THE SURFACE - Sam Lawson Mystery 2

DARK HARBOR - Sam Lawson Mystery 3

DEADLY REPUTATION - Sam Lawson Mystery 4

Also by David K. Wilson:
RED DIRT BLUES

Learn more at davidkwilsonauthor.com

ACKNOWLEDGMENTS

Thank YOU for taking the time to read my books. I hope you enjoy them and I can continue to entertain you. That said, I would not be able to do any of this without a small group of incredible people.

Big thanks go to fellow authors **Lorraine Evanoff, Barbara Fournier, Yvonne Pelletier** and **James Hewitson.** Your ideas, insights and suggestions always help improve my books.

Super big shout-out goes to **Regina Riddle** and **Rena Grubbs,** or as I call them, the Wonder Sisters. I've grown to trust their instincts and eagle eyes so much, and their support along the way helps ease the tediousness of writing and rewriting and rewriting and rewriting.

Heartfelt thanks to fellow Texan expatriate **Shelley Upchurch** for your support, suggestions and stories (that may or may not fuel future characters).

I also have to thank all of those who have helped spread the word of my books to help me grow my reader base, led by my dear friend and unofficial promotions manager **Jo-Ann Lant.**

Finally, a big thank you to my family who inspire me every day.

ABOUT THE AUTHOR

David K. Wilson grew up in East Texas, surrounded by enough colorful characters to fill the pages of hundreds of books. In addition to being the author of the popular Sam Lawson Mystery series, David is also a seasoned ghostwriter and screenwriter. He currently lives in upstate New York.

Sign up to receive news and information about David's next novel at davidkwilsonauthor.com.

facebook.com/davidkwilsonauthor

instagram.com/davidkwilsonauthor

goodreads.com/davidkwilson

www.ingramcontent.com/pod-product-compliance
Lightning Source LLC
Chambersburg PA
CBHW030820210726
48290CB00002B/680